otherworld

Erin E.M. Hatton

A Novel

OTHERWORLD

ISBN-13: 978-1-77069-221-3

Word Alive Press
131 Cordite Road, Winnipeg, MB R3W 1S1
www.wordalivepress.ca

WORD ALIVE PRESS
Just Write!

Library and Archives Canada Cataloguing in Publication

Hatton, Erin, 1978-
    Otherworld / Erin E.M. Hatton.

ISBN 978-1-77069-221-3

    I. Title.

PS8615.A783O85 2010   C813'.6   C2010-907893-4

Dedicated to my heavenly husband and my earthly one—
Who have both taught me so much about enduring love.

My favourite fairy tale was always Sleeping Beauty. The idea of a dashing prince coming to the rescue of a damsel in distress appealed to me, for obvious reasons. But I always wondered...what if the prince got there and the princess wasn't as beautiful as he thought?

1

The first time I saw him, I didn't think that much of him. He seemed a little awkward, like the types who sometimes wander into our part of the city by accident. He might not have been looking, but I was always up for a challenge. With a calculated smile, I tucked my hair behind my ear and drew my fingertips down my neck to rest on my shoulder.

"You lost?" I asked.

"I'm looking for someone," he said with a frown. He had nice eyebrows, I remember thinking. Heavy, dark, but not neanderthalish. He was tall and handsome, with brown hair, a strong, square jaw, a lean but broad build. Best of all, he had deep-set, sensitive eyes. I always paid attention to eyes. In hindsight, I think that's because I was always looking for something there—a spark that said "I'm alive!" I hadn't found it before, not in the stone-dead eyes of Lucas's thugs, nor in the haunted eyes of my usual patrons, not until that day.

That took me aback, seeing the aliveness in his eyes. But I was an actress. I had to be in my line of work. So I didn't show any trace of surprise. I did my best slinky walk in a half-circle around him, forcing him to turn to keep up with me. He did, but there was something different about the way he responded. Not lewd, like other men. Not at all. His eyes stayed on my face.

"Who are you looking for in a place like this?" I prodded.

A second glance confirmed my original guess that he wasn't from around here. He was well dressed, if a bit simply, in a black leather jacket, striped t-shirt, and jeans. The shoes gave it away—nice leather affairs from some designer store.

"Would you believe, my true love?" he said with a laugh.

I laughed indulgently. "I could be your true love, for a price." I raised my eyebrow.

He took a long, appraising look. Not the kind of look other men would give me, raking their eyes from neck to toes and back again. No, he stared deep into my eyes, delving beneath the surface. Looking for something. I dropped my gaze, for once shaken.

"No," he said softly. "Not the price I had in mind."

I pouted, unaccountably angered by the stranger's slight. "Well, a girl's got to eat, you understand. If you'll excuse me ..." A car was purring by, and if this guy wasn't buying, I might still flag this other one down.

He gave a lopsided smile and put up his hands in surrender. "Alright, I won't bother you. But I didn't mean anything by it, you know. I'm waiting for *her*." The car moved on. I cursed silently, then turned back to the man. I was curious enough not to be angry.

"This girl, has she got a name? I could keep an eye out for her."

He smiled. "She wouldn't remember the name I know. She must have a new one now."

I caught sight of a movement across the street. Sloane was coming to chase this guy away so other buyers wouldn't scare off. Belatedly, I realized I was in trouble. The stranger had a talent for capturing attention, but I couldn't afford to be distracted.

"Hey, listen," I said brusquely. "I'd love to chat all day, but I've got a job to do, so if you're not interested ..."

"Ah, yes," he said. What was that emotion in his eyes? Embarrassment? Judgement? Pity? Although it looked like any of these, I didn't get the feeling it really was. To my surprise, he pulled out his wallet. Funny, he didn't seem the buying type.

Surprised, I took the bills he put in my hand. "Let's go somewhere," I said, shaking my head to ward off Sloane and turning on the toes of my stilettos.

"No need," he said. "I'm merely paying you for the time I've taken up. Wouldn't want to cause any trouble for you."

"Are you some kind of cop?" I asked, squinting my eyes at him. I didn't know whether or not to be insulted.

He laughed. "If I was I'd have already slapped cuffs on you. No...I'm just a guy looking for his lost love." He looked away down the street, but his eyes seemed to look further, to some point invisible from where we stood.

I didn't really want to shoo him away, as intrigued as I was, but Sloane gave me a glare, and I sighed.

"Oh...alright. Good luck with that," I said. I turned my back on whatever good bye he might have given. But I did look back over my shoulder to watch him walk away.

I had thought him awkward, but he wasn't. It was me that was awkward, out of place. It wasn't that he didn't belong in my part of town. It was as if he carried a world with him of which I was not a part. For a wistful moment, I wanted to be.

—

"That's a good take, Emma," Lucas Fulbright said with a smile on his devilishly handsome face. Glints of grey amid the dark of his hair sparked in the light cast by the old warehouse lamps. He inclined his muscular frame back in the chair with the confident poise of a man who owned the world. As well he might, since he practically did. He was one of the richest, most powerful men in all the earth, even if he'd had to sell his soul to get there.

He waved the wad of bills in front of him, letting them fan back and forth impressively. "Best thing I ever did, taking you in as a kid. If half of you girls could do in a week what Emma did tonight, you'd be in much better shape. As it is, Holly, you practically cost me money out there tonight. You'll not be getting your bit this morning. Sloane, take Emma to her room and make sure you take good care of her. Holly, I'll deal with you personally."

With a pleased smile, Sloane ushered me towards the back of the big storage room that served as Lucas's office. He was pleased because he would be well rewarded for making sure I worked hard. My room was a small converted office upstairs in the warehouse. It was a hole in the wall—little more than a cubicle—but it was better than most. It was private, for starters. I ranked a big real bed instead of a camp cot, and a goose down duvet, though it had no cover. I had a few changes of clothes and a dresser with a mirror, and my own table with two chairs. I was good at my job, and the good ones got the perks.

Good care in our outfit meant a few things. I got a nice hot shower—the best girls got to shower first, and used up all the hot water. I got a better breakfast, too. But most of all, it meant Ambrosia. That was worth more than the shower and the breakfast and the bed put together. I could do without food, sleep, maybe even oxygen as long as I got Ambrosia. I didn't know what it was, really. Probably some kind of heroin hybrid. I only know I was raised on it like mother's milk, and I couldn't live without it.

There were some nights I didn't do well enough, and I was denied my dose. Those were the darkest days, where I lay in waking nightmares, shaking in the broken bars of light that came through my closed curtains. I did my best to make sure those nights were few and far between, so I would never have to feel that way again.

I rushed through my shower and breakfast, barely noticing the steaming hot water and the delicious food. I put on the first thing I pulled from my drawer, a worn red silky robe with a small hole developing on the seam.

My last client had been a latecomer—a slow one at that—and I felt the need of Ambrosia keenly after the wait. It was like a dark haze at first that leached what little enjoyment existed in my world. If this was ignored—and this would only ever be forcibly, for no one would voluntarily endure it—the longing became more insistent, like a mist that becomes a strangling monster. The beast of addiction blotted out all other thoughts, until satiated.

Impatient, I waited for Sloane to return to my room. I was tapping my black-manicured fingernails on the table with a sound that would have been annoying to me, had I not been so preoccupied.

At last, Sloane came in with a negligent knock never meant to be answered. He pulled out the other chair, twirling it around so he could straddle the back. I'd never known him to sit in a chair properly.

"Alright, girl," he said gruffly, pushing up his sleeves over burly tattooed forearms. He eyed my tapping fingers with a grim look. "Don't get your knickers in a twist." He pulled out a zippered case, seeming to take forever as he slipped out a filled syringe. My arm was already laid on the table, face up. I didn't even notice the prick of the needle. Some of the newer girls said the injections bothered them, but for me, it was a part of life, no more notable than clipping one's toenails.

"Sleep well, princess," Sloane said with a smile, zipping up the case and tapping it gently on the table before sliding it into his pocket and standing. I headed for the bed before I lost track of where I was.

Rolling over between the sheets, I curled my knees up against my chest and stared at the wall. This was the worst part—the waiting. It was the time between, when the longing had been answered and the drug not yet taken effect. It was the moment of clarity for me, that brief window where I was alone with my true thoughts.

Sometimes I wondered about my history—my unremembered parents, the childhood I must have had. I thought about Lucas, sometimes thankful he took me in, more often cursing him. This morning, though, it was the stranger's face that came to me.

He intrigued me more than I had let myself think. He was eye–catching, certainly, and to be attracted to someone in my line of work was a rare pleasure. But it was more than the obvious physical side of things. I couldn't shake the attraction of his personality. I felt as though I had seen a glimpse of his soul—his beautiful, multi–faceted soul. It was something I had never imagined existed.

But as surely as he had shown me his soul, he had seen mine. I felt as though he had examined every black and twisted part of me when he'd looked so long into my eyes. Now that I was here in my bed, away from the glamour and bravado of my act, my eyes started with sudden tears. I dashed them away with anger at my weakness. He didn't know me—let him try to judge!

But I knew it wasn't the stranger judging me. It was me. That was the other thing I thought about before the Ambrosia took its hold. After the puzzle of my past, the hate–love I felt for Lucas, and whatever interesting event that came my way in the course of a night on the street, the guilt always came like a landslide that covered all else.

It was bad enough on a normal morning, when all I had to hold up against my life was the gritty underworld of Lucas's kingdom. But today it was unbearable. Today I had seen a thing that negated all my flimsy comparisons. I knew beyond doubt now that there was something good and pure, a touchstone to aspire to, a mirror to show me my faults. There was a bright world that stood as a foil for my dark shadow life. And the stranger embodied it.

His face was the last thing I remembered—with more clarity even than memories of people I'd known all my life—before the Ambrosia took me in its pleasant arms of oblivion.

—

It was two in the morning when I slid my legs out of the car onto the slick street. Raining. Ugh. Hopefully it wouldn't be long before I was out of the rain again. I caught Sloane's eye with a reassuring glance and took up my post as the car drove away with a swish of water from a puddle. He looked back with some indefinable expression. I followed the gruff tilt of his chin, and it was then that I saw the figure leaning against the streetlight across the road.

His brown hair was spiked with rain, but I recognized him at once. The stranger. My heart did an uneven two-step until I willed my lungs to exhale again. Stupid girl, I told myself, even as I fought to control the smile that rose as he pushed away from the post and strolled across the shiny black pavement.

Sloane recognized him too, I could tell by his expression. He half rose from his seat under an awning nearby, but I waved him off. The man was close enough now that I could see his face. He had a little half smile that I couldn't quite read. I didn't know why he'd come back, but some part of me was ridiculously elated that he had.

"Came back for more?" I was unable to resist. To be honest, I hoped he had come back for more than just talk.

"More of your company, at least." He raised his eyes to the teeming rain, and drops glistened in his dark eyelashes. "Nice evening, isn't it?"

I lifted an eyebrow with a puzzled laugh. "I've seen nicer weather, and two in the morning doesn't exactly count as evening anymore."

"I don't suppose it does."

"So you'd like my company?" I prodded, looking up through my own now-wet eyelashes.

"Hmmm. How about some coffee, or is that too suburban for you?"

I laughed out loud this time. "No, I enjoy coffee from time to time." Then my face fell slightly. "Of course ..."

"I wouldn't dream of taking your time without compensation, Miss ..." he let his words hang like a question.

"Delaney," I answered without hesitation. "Emma Delaney." Now that was odd. I never gave my own name out to a client. Sometimes it was Sugar, or something innocent like Sarah or Jane, or dark and mysterious like Natasha. Sometimes it was a name the client supplied. Most often it was no name at all. But never, ever Emma. And certainly never Delaney. What was it about this guy?

He pulled out a sizeable wad of bills and passed it to me. No quick, shifty, shame-filled exchange. No ostentatious flaunting that demanded extra services. He put it in my hand matter-of-factly and smiled.

"For the pleasure of your time, Miss Delaney."

"Emma, please."

"Emma." There was a strange look in his eyes as he said my name—a soft pain that astonished me.

He held out his arm, and I shook away the thought. Suddenly, I wanted to know his name. I'd never cared before. "Coffee, then, Mr. ..." I fished, stashing the money in my bustier and putting my hand through the crook of his elbow like we were a courting couple in the olden days.

"Kynsey," he replied, seeming pleased. "Cale Kynsey."

He took me into the little all-night diner just down the street, and we had to pass by Sloane's bench on the way. The burly man's eyebrows nearly went up to his hairline, if he'd had any hair. Then he shrugged as if to say "you know what you're doing, kid." I could only imagine what he was thinking when we turned into the diner.

The fluorescent lights and cheery music were a little off-putting after what I was used to. A waitress came to take our order, the kind of woman who looked like she was thirty but was probably eighteen. I guessed she had a couple of little kids at home she was raising by herself. She looked weary.

Cale ordered coffee for us both, and pie, kindly inquiring what I would like. No one had asked me that in a long time. He thanked the waitress warmly, and I noticed that she walked a little straighter when she left.

Silence fell over the table, and Cale leaned back comfortably in his seat, smiling at me.

"So, any luck finding your true love?" I asked with a light laugh, awkward under his scrutiny. I flipped my chin–length hair and fluffed the rain out of my bangs, taking off my wet trench coat and laying it over the back of the seat.

"I think so," he said, still just short of staring. I noticed in the light that his eyes were grey–green.

"That's good," I said with a detached air. It was the farthest thing from what I really felt. The thought of this man with someone else made me sick. That was a first.

"Trouble is I don't think she remembers me."

"How could she not remember you?" I scoffed.

He shrugged. "Don't know. She's been through a lot. Changed."

"Is she still your 'true love', then?" I asked, unable to keep the slight scornful edge out of the words.

The waitress returned with the coffee, pie and a smile, interrupting our conversation for the moment. It might have been my imagination, but it seemed like the dark circles under her eyes had faded a bit. I dismissed the thought and turned back to Cale, pointedly ignoring the coffee and pie until he answered my question. I didn't know why, but I deeply cared to know the answer.

"Is she?" I asked, more softly.

He smiled sadly, hinting at a wealth of pain beneath the surface. "Of course she is. It doesn't matter how much she changes or what has been done to her, or even what *she* has done. I will always love her, because she will always *be* her." His eyes were intense, and I looked away. My cheeks burned.

Was it jealousy I felt? Anger? Shame? Hope? I didn't know. It was all new territory tonight.

"Sounds very noble," I said. All of the above, I decided, on the emotions poll. "And what about your girl? Does she still love you?" I bit my lip in suspense.

"I don't know," Cale said, finally looking down at the cup of coffee he cradled in his hands. A drop of water fell from his spiked hair to the table, and he lifted the cup to his lips. I followed suit.

"Do you think that's fair to you?" I asked at last.

"It's not about fairness. I love her." He took a little bit of his pie. "If you want to talk about fairness, what about her? It breaks my heart to see what she's been through."

I ignored his considerations. "How did you get separated in the first place?" I asked. "I mean, if she's really your true love, why did you let each other go?"

He looked out the window at the rain-soaked street. "Sorry," he muttered, and I could see moisture in his eyes. "It happened a very long time ago, but it still feels fresh." He looked me in the eye frankly. "She ran off with my best friend—or my worst enemy—I'm not sure how to explain it."

"Well, you've paid me enough that I could sit here for the next three nights ..." I offered.

"Really?" he said with a laugh. "I've been gouged! No, truly—I don't begrudge the money. Okay, you want to hear it?"

I nodded, lacing my fingers together under my chin and adopting a look of rapt attention. "So which is it? Best friend or worst enemy? So far I vote for the latter."

"He *was* my best friend, you could say. My wing man. There was nobody else I trusted more. But then things began to go sour. He got jealous, I guess. He kept trying to sabotage me. It was subtle, at first, but eventually I had to say something. He didn't take it well. He did everything he could to destroy all that I'd built after that point.

"Then...*she* came along. She was everything to me. Everything." He stopped for a second, taking a sip of coffee with closed eyes. I stared at him, enthralled. Just for once, I'd like to be someone's everything.

"And he took her from you?"

He opened his eyes. "He didn't just take her. He turned her against me. First it was just little seeds of doubt. She began to question if I had her best interests at heart, if I really loved her. He promised her things. Big things. Then, one day, she was gone."

"I'm sorry."

"You know the real shame of it?" he asked with haunted eyes. "I would have given her so much more than he lured her away with. And I would have been okay if he had kept his promise. But I know for a fact he's abused her in so many ways there's not a piece of her left he hasn't ruined."

I listened in stunned silence, not sure what to say.

"We were engaged, you know?" His voice was so low it was almost a whisper. "I was going to marry her."

"What will you do now?" I asked, matching his whisper.

"I plan to woo her back, no matter what it takes, if she'll have me."

"What if she won't?" I insisted. I still didn't like the idea of another woman having him, especially a woman who'd betrayed him. But I found I did care enough about Cale to want his happiness.

"She'll have to make that perfectly clear to me. If there's any chance—any chance at all that she could come back to me, then I'll do everything in my power to win her back."

"Why would you do that after what she did to you?" I was angry now.

"You don't understand," he said patiently, his eyes burning into mine. "I promised her, when he took her away. I saw the look in her eyes when she understood what he was, and what she had given up. She was sorry. She was terrified! I knew I couldn't just let her leave and forget her. She needs me."

"Maybe so," I muttered. He was stubborn. I realized I didn't want him to be any other way. If everlasting love could exist, this was it. And if he gave up on this mysterious woman, then it wasn't that kind of love—and I wanted so badly to know it was real, even if it wasn't mine.

"What about you," Cale asked, looking up at me over his mug.

"What about me?" I asked evasively.

"Well, what's your story?"

"Not much of one, I'm afraid," I replied, glancing out the window and back to my plate. "Tell the truth, I don't remember my childhood. Probably too traumatic to remember."

Cale nodded once as though this made sense to him, folding his hands so his two index fingers rested against his lips. I took this as an invitation to go on.

"As far as I know from what people have told me, Lucas found me on the street as a teenager and took me in."

"Lucas Fulbright." It wasn't a question. Cale knew more about the underworld than I gave him credit for. He said the name in a way that implied he knew everything there was to know about the man, and he didn't think much of him.

"He gave me a roof over my head, and food. Protected me. And he gave me a living," I added defensively.

"Of sorts," Cale said quietly.

I smiled without humour. "It's not something a rich pretty boy could understand."

He held my eyes for a moment, and I thought he might be the only one who really *did* understand.

"Are you happy, Emma?" he asked.

I hesitated, glancing out the window again. The rain had stopped.

"What's happy?" I evaded. "You hear about these rich execs who have everything that's supposed to make you happy, and they're not. I don't know that happy is realistic."

"I guess not," he said with a chuckle. "Not in this world, anyway. Okay, then, let me rephrase the question. If you could change your life, would you?"

I took a bite of pie to fill the space before I answered. What was I supposed to say? Yeah, in a heartbeat. I mean, who would *choose* a life like mine? But I couldn't tell him that every once in a while, a sort of window would open to my soul, letting in a stream of brilliant hope along with the sights, sounds, and smells of my own unreachable paradise.

"It's complicated." It was a cliché, but it was all I could say.

"Are you in trouble?" he asked, looking at me with genuine concern from under his brows.

"No, no, nothing like that. I'm pretty sure if I went to Lucas and told him I wanted out, he'd let me. He wouldn't be happy, but he'd let me."

"I wouldn't be so sure," Cale mused, almost to himself.

"Well, I can't say I know. I've never asked. But he took me in, after all. Doesn't that earn some kind of loyalty?" That was the only way I could explain. I couldn't tell him about the Ambrosia, and how it bound me to Lucas more securely than iron chains. There were many different kinds of loyalty. My little window on paradise slammed shut, bringing back to mind my true surroundings.

I felt it all fall back into place around me—the stale, stagnant air, the drone of a dozen machines, the cold fluorescent light, and the endless succession of faceless men in my foreseeable future. After the foreseeable, there was only blankness. I couldn't, or wouldn't, go there, to the time when age ended my usefulness. This was my reality, enforced by the Ambrosia.

Then a warm hand covered mine. I didn't flinch. I was used to touch, even from strangers. He'd paid for more than that, after all.

"The way I understand loyalty," he said softly, "Is that it's freely given, by definition."

I wanted to deny his implication, that I wasn't loyal by choice. But it wouldn't be the truth, and for some strange reason, I was all about the truth tonight. Even if I had lied, I was sure he would have seen right through it.

15

"Maybe you're right," I said with a shrug. "But it doesn't change anything." I gave him a frank look, almost a glare. He gazed back–calmly, but not impassively. There was a depth of strong emotion beneath the smoothness of his expression that startled me. I looked away, to the fog that was forming in swirling patterns under the streetlights.

His hand was still covering mine, and his thumb stroked my skin. It surprised me—not the touch itself, but the fact that it seemed so *normal*. It was comforting and harmless and completely devoid of demand, unlike any touch I had experienced in my limited memory. Without thinking, I squeezed his fingers gently in return. It was my way of telling him what I could not say.

"It's stopped raining," I said, turning back. "And the coffee's gone."

"If you want to get back ..."

"I probably should," I mused. "It would be great money. But then again...I don't have to." I laid a hand over my décolletage where his fee rested.

"Apparently not," he said with a laugh. "How about a walk?"

"Why not?" I pushed my dishes away and slid out of the booth, reaching for my cropped trench coat. But it was whisked out of my hands before I could say anything, and when I turned around, Cale was holding it out for me, Ward Cleaver–style. I looked at him in surprise for a moment, then with a shrug, turned my back to him and slipped my arms in the sleeves. As he put the jacket on, his hands rested briefly on my shoulders. Again, the touch was warm and pleasant, but nothing more.

16

The waitress rang our bill through. I let Cale pay, partly habit, partly self-preservation, and partly because I knew this was a drop in the bucket compared to the money he'd thrown at me the last two nights for nothing. When he was done, I turned to leave, but he hung back. Curious, I looked back over my shoulder.

"You're doing a good job, you know," Cale was saying softly to the waitress, barely loud enough for me to hear. "Your kids know you love them. You're a good mother."

The waitress had been about to shut the till, but she froze mid-motion. To my surprise, tears started in her eyes, and she stared at Cale. For a long moment she read his eyes, searching for sincerity as I had done. At last, she smiled, with a quick, breaking half-sob, half-laugh.

"Thank you," she whispered.

"Have a good night," he said, and passed something to her. Money, I thought.

He offered his arm to me, and I took it again. As we went outside into the cool, misty air, I turned to him.

"How did you know to do that?"

He shrugged. "I have a talent for understanding people."

"But why? Are you in the random acts of kindness business?" I asked. "Racking up the brownie points?" I immediately regretted my words.

I thought he'd be offended, but he smiled instead, like he was laughing at a private joke. "Random acts of kindness, yes. I suppose you could say it's my business. But brownie points, no. I don't feel the need to impress anyone. You could call it gratitude—pay-it-forward and all that."

"Fair enough. I guess I shouldn't complain, being a recipient of your generosity." I felt sheepishly resentful that I was just another charity case to him.

"It's a little more than that," he said, looking down at me. "... with you."

I stopped walking, and he didn't seem to mind. He turned his whole length to face me, though he didn't step any closer. I almost expected him to.

"Okay, here's the thing." I held up my hands. "I don't understand why you're doing this. Giving the waitress a couple of bucks because she's down on her luck—I understand that. Quick, easy, simple. But me? First you're looking for your long lost fairy tale princess, so I get that you needed help. I listened to your story—and if you ask me, that woman of yours isn't worth the trouble. But I respect the kind of love you've got. I do. Yet now here you go saying that it's *different* with *me*? What am I supposed to think about that? Are you that fickle? You'll do anything to win her back, but you'll diddle with me in the meantime?"

I was a little angrier than maybe I should have been. I wanted to stalk away, with my tall heels clicking neatly on the sidewalk. But I was more interested in hearing his answer.

"You're a clever woman, Emma," he said gently. "I'm sure you can puzzle it out."

Ideas were spinning in my head like the tumblers of a lock. I could almost hear the snick of the little metal pieces falling into place. A lost love found—just after he met me. A faulty memory—just like mine. A jealous, abusive captor—and a corresponding crime boss.

"Me? You think it's *me*?" I shrilled, caught between confusion, anger, and oddly enough, regret. His logic was faulty.

It couldn't be me. "You're insane! First of all, okay, Lucas isn't some archenemy. He's not the greatest guy in the world, but he didn't steal me away or abuse me. I know I don't remember a lot, but I'm certain I've never met you before in my life! How could I possibly be your long lost fiancée?"

"You'd rather I left you alone?" he asked. His voice was soft and calm as always, but I could see by the tension in his jaw and the intensity of his eyes that he cared very deeply about the outcome of this discussion.

"No," I said with a sigh. I turned away and went on walking, not away from him, but inviting him to come along. "I like you, Cale," I admitted. "I like spending time with you. In fact, this is the best night I've had in a long time. But I'm not who you want. I can't even pretend to be that. Could you see me as a wife? Even if I...wanted to leave Lucas ..."

Cale's silence was awkward. I was afraid to look at him, worried that I had hurt him, even though the whole idea was crazy. The shameful truth was that I did very much want it to be true. I knew at that moment that I would gladly run away with him and be his wife—that I could be as long as he made it real. Being with him was like a whole other world. But there was the Ambrosia that would always stand between us. I couldn't give it up.

"Listen," I said, as much to myself as to him. "I can't be what you want. I'm not that girl." I sounded harsh, even in my own ears. Dropping the tough act, I let him see an uncharacteristically vulnerable face. "But I'm much too selfish to tell you to go away. I like you a lot. Besides, you're my best customer." I smiled with a shrug to soften the words. I met his eyes then, and regretted it. Pain emanated from him, though

I could tell he tried to hide it. But in the midst of it, I could see a bright spark of optimistic determination. I remembered what he'd said: that as long as there was hope, he would do whatever it took to win her...*me*. I knew it was true. Despite everything, I hoped very much he would succeed.

2

Cale walked with me for the rest of the night, until dawn coloured the fog with a rose red light that suggested more bad weather to come. We didn't talk much, at my request. We just enjoyed what time we had left. But the meter was ticking away, and time was up. He walked me back to Sloane and said goodbye, said he'd see me that night. There was nothing in his outward demeanour that hinted at the turmoil I guessed and hoped he felt within—the same that I felt.

Sloane looked at me, bristling with curiosity. I pulled out my money and dropped it in his hand in explanation.

"Hmm," he grunted in surprise at the money before he pocketed it. "And he didn't ...?"

"Not so much as a peck on the cheek," I said with a shrug. "Easiest money I ever made. Do you think it's okay?"

"Why wouldn't it be? You got paid, didn't you? As long as the guy doesn't damage you, who cares what a paying customer chooses to do with his time. As far as I'm concerned, you deserve a little break, princess."

He draped a companionable arm around my shoulders, making me feel like a frail little doll in comparison to his bulk. Sloane was the only man in my life who had never seemed to want me for something else, and I was grateful. For a girl without a father, this man was it.

Sloane walked me in the direction of Lucas's warehouse.

"Saw you having a bit of a tiff with that gent not too long ago. Everything alright?" he asked.

"Yeah," I said, knowing Sloane wouldn't be fully convinced. I had to elaborate. "He thought I was someone he knew a long time ago. Big misunderstanding. I think we have it cleared up now."

"I've never seen you so riled about anything. You been keeping your professional distance?" He sounded concerned.

"Yes," I said irritably. Truth be told, I wasn't. I had been careless to let Cale get under my skin the way he had. I should have told him to get lost, if I'd known what was good for me. In as long as I could remember, I had never, ever, got angry with a customer. Sure, I had pretended enough times, but for real...did that mean I was falling for Cale?

I thought carefully about the past hours. Although romantic love wasn't a welcome part of my world, I was no stranger to it. There had been one or two clients whose company I had enjoyed as much as they had mine. When they came for me, I was thrilled. When they stayed away, disappointed. But it was never more than a little infatuation. I had never cared enough to get mad.

Cale had reached my emotions on an unprecedented level. I wasn't sure I liked it. But I was already in too deep to make him stay away. That was a bad sign. I sighed.

"Okay, no," I admitted to Sloane. "But I'm not going to do anything stupid. Don't worry."

"Fine," he said. "I trust you. You're the toughest, smartest girl I know. I'll keep it to myself. But if I see things going ugly...I'm going to have to step in."

"You won't have to," I promised as he opened the door of

Lucas's warehouse for me.

—

A present was waiting for me on my bed when I got out of the shower that morning. I tugged the ribbon and let the tissue paper fall open, revealing a neatly folded black silk something. I held it up appraisingly, half–delighted and half–aloof. I didn't feel like I needed a reward simply for spending time in Cale's company. But any girl would still appreciate a gift.

It was a long night gown, elegant, but slinky, with a few beaded details and velvet trims that gave it a hint of nostalgia. Lucas's style, alright. I put it on, relishing the feel of the silk against my clean skin. I had come back a shade early, so I wasn't feeling the lack of Ambrosia quite yet. I enjoyed my breakfast, and took a minute to fix myself up in the mirror.

I tried not to obsess about my looks. It ruined the confidence. Despite the grooming and the dieting, there were always things I didn't like, so I avoided deep inspection in the mirror at all times. But right now, with thoughts of my time with Cale fresh in my mind, I wanted to look, to see what he had seen.

I saw my face staring back at me, although no matter how many times I saw it, it always surprised me. How silly that was, to find my own face foreign. I looked strikingly beautiful on first glance, with my dark mahogany hair slicked back with the wet, and my pale oval face with its wide, slightly tilted blue eyes, delicate nose, arched brows, and sensual lips. The body was even better—long, slender, just the right combination of firm and soft. I liked the new gown on me, and I turned myself about to get a look from every angle.

Makeup usually served to enhance the image, with seductive cat-eye liner and crimson lip gloss. Right now, though, after my shower, the makeup was gone, and my hair beginning to fly up in little wisps. On closer inspection, I saw the dark circles under my eyes, the blemishes lurking beneath my skin, the bulge just under my hip, and the little crooked skew to the left brow, usually hidden under my bangs. Irritably, I fluffed my bangs back into place, reaching for a comb to tame my hair.

The door opened, but I didn't turn at first. For some reason, I suddenly cared what I looked like.

"Just a minute, Sloane," I said.

"You look beautiful. I thought it would suit you."

I whirled, dropping the comb. It wasn't Sloane at all, but Lucas. I relaxed again, moving to the table.

"Thank you," I said. Lucas carried the little pack of syringes, and he pulled one out for me. I laid my arm on the table, noticing for the first time in a while the faint needle tracks on the pale skin. I looked away, wondering what Cale would think of this flaw. My own words rang out accusingly in my head: *If you ask me, that woman of yours isn't worth the trouble.*

Although I wasn't the one he thought I was, I felt ashamed. If I *had* been his lost love—and the thing that made me nervous was I couldn't truthfully say if I was or not, because I had no memory of the past—I had been an awful one. I couldn't see how he could want me as I really was, let alone thinking I had done those things to him.

"You did well last night," Lucas interrupted my self-deprecation in a voice that was almost a purr. He stood up, but showed no signs of leaving. Instead, he came over behind where I was sitting and stroked his fingers through my damp hair. I closed my eyes. Usually, I would have enjoyed the sensation. Today I felt sick at his touch. Odd.

"Thank you," I murmured.

"I like this hair colour on you."

"I can't even remember what my real hair colour is anymore."

Lucas chuckled. He bent down and kissed the back of my neck.

It wasn't often that Lucas visited me. But it had happened on occasion. He was decent, and handsomer than most, if a bit old, so I didn't mind. It was my job, after all. And though I didn't get paid when it was Lucas, I looked at it as room and board. In fact, if I was really honest, I was usually flattered by the attention. At least if no one loved me, I could pretend desire was love.

But this morning, it seemed more onerous than before. Contrasted with Cale's unstoppable love for his lost woman, Lucas's attentions seemed like a bad counterfeit. After spending the night in innocence with Cale, this act seemed cheap and dirty. I held back the sigh that bubbled up under my ribs. I'd have to get over that attitude in a hurry, if I was to survive. I stood and turned to Lucas in one movement, playing the expected part as I looked up at him under my lashes.

He was dressed in his customary business suit, though he was loosening his tie. He bent his face to me with its keen blue eyes, crow's feet and all, and his well-shaped lips. But when I looked at Lucas's short-cropped, greying dark hair and lithe form, I could only compare him to Cale. That was a very, very bad sign, I thought, as I reluctantly accepted Lucas's kiss.

—

It was close to sunset, I could feel. I was alone, awake in bed. My knees were pulled close to my chest, my face wet, the new night-gown on the floor under the bed. I doubted I'd wear it again. I had slept for a while, after Lucas left, but I woke frequently, in the grip of Ambrosia-driven hallucinations. They were vague, but disquieting, and I had the impression that Cale figured prominently in them.

I was excited to see Cale again soon. That killed me. I had no right to want to be with him, no place beside him. I was only wasting his time. But I couldn't help it. He had gotten to me, as evidenced by my reaction to Lucas. He might have even ruined me for other men. That would make my job a living hell.

The problem wasn't seeing Cale. It wasn't even my sudden revulsion for Lucas. The problem was that I had admitted to myself a possibility, however small, that he might be right... about me, about Lucas, about everything.

My thoughts were a mess, made only worse by the waning effects of the Ambrosia. My lack of memory niggled at me more than ever, the unknown variables taunting me. I had assumed I'd had parents, probably irresponsible ones who had abandoned me. But what if I'd had a good life before? What if I had been loved and wanted?

If Lucas had stolen me away, he most certainly wouldn't tell me that, I admitted. If he really was as evil as Cale inferred, the first thing he would have done is lie to me about my past. Was it possible that he had somehow erased my memory, too? I couldn't begin to imagine how he might have done it.

I strained my mind to try to capture some stray memory of that time, as I so often tried to do. No luck. So, in place of that blank history, I spun a story for myself, based on what Cale had told me. I spent quite a while imagining a time when he and I were together. It was pleasant, with honeyed sunshine beaming down on the proverbial picket-fenced house. There were flowers and chocolates, like in the movies, and kisses. Oh, the kisses I imagined him giving me! There was a sparkling diamond ring on my left-hand fourth finger.

Idly, I rubbed my fingertips in a ring-shaped motion around that finger now, trying to see if it felt right. That was silly. If I had worn his ring, it was much too long ago to recall now. My empty finger reminded me of the rest of his story. The ring given back in anger, along with a betrayal so awful I couldn't imagine anyone bouncing back from it. I clenched my left hand into a fist around my empty finger, clasping it to my heart with my right hand. Fresh tears ran down my face and soaked my pillow.

It was a reality I couldn't accept, at least not without great pain. If I had loved him once, then I had also left him. I couldn't have the one without the other.

The door to my room opened, and I dashed the tears away with the back of my hand.

"I'm awake," I croaked softly.

"Rough sleep, princess?" Sloane asked in a sympathetic tone.

I answered with a humourless laugh. He withdrew quietly to let me get ready. Reluctantly, I rolled over and crawled out of bed, rubbing my eyes. It would take a lot of makeup to cover up the day's sleeplessness. I spent more time than I should have rummaging through my drawers for something good to wear. I had plenty of clothes, but I wanted something just right. Something pure enough for Cale. That was a joke.

In the end, I settled for a blue silk blouse, though I buttoned it up a little higher than usual. It was strange to feel modesty, even just a little. It had been so long since I had cared, if I ever had. The length of the skirt couldn't be helped. I did my hair soft and wavy tonight, instead of straight, and left the dark eyeliner in the drawer. With a little work, I looked fresh and sweet. More like the girl Cale deserved. At least, I *looked* more like that girl.

With a sigh, I pushed away from my dresser and went in search of dinner. As usual, I kept to myself, away from the other girls, though I noticed in a detached way that Holly, the girl with the poor track record, was gone. Fired, I guessed. I had never really bothered to know any of the other girls, I thought with a twinge of regret. Come to think of it, Lucas had never really encouraged—in fact almost discouraged—the others to fraternize with me. It made for a lonely life.

Sloane brought his plate over to me. At least I could count on him.

"Lookin' good, princess," he said with a smile. "What are you going for tonight? Innocent school girl?"

I glared at him and went on eating without an answer.

"Ah, I see. Well, why not, when he pays you the way he does. Knowing what little I do of him, he should like it."

I accepted the compliment with a secret smile and went on eating, aware of Sloane's watchful eyes studying me, but not acknowledging them. I knew what he was thinking, or worrying about, and it rankled the most that he was right. I was thinking far too much about Cale Kynsey.

As soon as I was finished a reasonable amount of my dinner, I abandoned my plate and rose. It was still early, so the other girls either stared in surprise or glared at me for being such an overachiever. It didn't matter. There was only one reason I would actually want to get to work early. Cale.

I brushed my teeth and touched up my lipstick, impatient with my slow and clumsy hands. Then I left, keeping a good two paces in front of Sloane in my eagerness. He didn't say anything, but I couldn't have known his thoughts more clearly if I was a telepath. When I reached my corner with its familiar lamppost, I began to pace back and forth, trying to calm myself to no avail. When a car rolled past, I shrank from the streetlight's circle into the anonymous shadows.

Sloane gave me a warning glance from his bench, but I glared back. If I wasn't sure that Cale was coming, I would never have made such a dangerous move. An hour passed, and I began to question my certainty. Would he come? A grey car purred to a halt beside me and the window rolled down. My heart began to race. What would I say? I couldn't very well refuse a client outright, or Lucas would have my head.

But when I saw the driver lean toward the passenger door, his face illuminated by the streetlight, my fears were erased. My heart was still hammering, but for a different reason now.

"Why, Mr. Kynsey," I said with the first genuine smile I'd had in years. "How kind of you to show up."

"Could I offer you a ride, Miss Delaney?" he asked, popping open the passenger door as he copied my mock-manners.

"Of course," I replied, sliding smoothly into the leather seat and closing the door. I was nervous. Would he like me? It was the first time I had been in a situation where my highly effective feminine wiles wouldn't override everything else.

"You look lovely, Emma," he said, gazing at me with the weight of truth in his eyes.

"Thank you. Where shall we go?"

"Anywhere you like, although I do know of a nice spot in a park with a view ..."

"Sounds great," I said. I wanted to add *unless you'd like some place more private*...but I stopped myself. I wasn't sure whether it was habit that made me want to say it, or something more. The rush of adrenaline made me think the latter. But I had to be careful with Cale. He was different.

Cale put the car into gear and pulled out onto the street.

"You've been crying," he said, without looking at me a second time. "Are you alright?"

"No one's been beating me, if that's what you're wondering," I said sarcastically to hide my shock. How did he know so easily? I checked myself quickly in the car's side mirror, but I didn't look like I'd been bawling my eyes out. At least, I didn't think so.

"Have you been thinking about what I said?" This time he did look at me, out of the corner of his eyes. He seemed to be testing my emotional stability.

"A little," I lied. I couldn't meet his eyes, or my casual façade would unravel.

"What do you think about it?"

"Hmm," I smiled. "Well, I still think it's completely insane. But I'm willing to have a little fun playing along. For example, hypothetically speaking, what would my name be?"

"Hmm?" he inquired, turning a corner.

"You know. When you first met me, you said your lost love had a different name that she wouldn't remember. What is it?"

He smiled with a single laugh. "I'm not sure you'd be able to pronounce it. But I can tell you your current name is very much like it—it means the same thing. I pay very close attention to names."

"Oh?"

"Yes. Emma means 'universal' in this language, although in our language it means more like 'everything'."

I shivered.

"And my last name?"

Cale lowered his chin, and his aspect seemed to darken drastically. "Yes, that. That was a later addition. It is very close to a word in our language that means 'Child of the Enemy'. I think it's a very sick joke. He either wants to mark you as belonging to him, or remind himself that you're supposed to belong to me. Or both. It all depends on who he is calling the Enemy."

"And by 'he' you mean Lucas?"

"Mmm hmm," he confirmed.

"This is crazy," I muttered, looking out the window. I didn't know what else I had expected, though I felt like I was descending into less than sane territory myself.

"And yet you want to know," Cale observed.

"I suppose that's true," I said with a sigh. "Well then, while we're playing hypothetical games, when did all of this happen? And why don't I remember any of it?"

"It's possible that it was all too traumatic, and you suppressed it, as you suggested," Cale mused in all seriousness. "But I think it's rather more likely that Lucas somehow wiped your memory."

I laughed it off, but the idea was uncomfortably close to what I had been thinking, just hours earlier. I was amazed at how seriously Cale discussed this whole fiasco. Either he was so delusional that this impossible story had become his reality, he was a very good liar, or it truly was real.

"Okay, but you didn't answer my question about the age factor. When did this happen?"

"A very, very long time ago. Can we leave it at that?" Cale was evasive for the first time, and I wondered what he was hiding.

"Fine."

We pulled up to the side of the road, and Cale came around to my door as I was getting out. He took my hand, holding my gaze as he raised me to the curb. I took a step onto the grass and my stiletto heel promptly sank three inches into the moist soil.

With a laugh, I wrenched it loose. "I guess these aren't the best shoes for walking in the park."

"Take them off, then," Cale said. He was already on his knees, undoing the buckle on the ankle strap. He tossed them into the car, and took off his own shoes and socks. "There's nothing like soft grass on bare feet. Come on."

He offered his hand this time, instead of his elbow, and I took it without hesitating. He was right—the grass did feel good, caressing my sore feet with cool moisture. I raised my eyes, across a tree–lined expanse of lawn. Right now it was silvery in the moonlight, but I imagined in the daytime it would be verdant gold–tipped green. At the far end of the lawn was an old stone wall with a bench before it, and beyond, an endless vista of sparkling city lights.

We could have been any couple, strolling across the grass hand in hand. I wanted to pretend that we were—that there was nothing complicating this moment. He led me to the bench and we sat down, basking in the beauty of the moonlit view and the quiet night sounds for a while in silence. I laid my head on Cale's shoulder. It was a simple, childlike gesture, and when he raised his arm to put it around me, I didn't complain.

We spent hours like that—snuggled together on the park bench. Every once in a while we would talk for a bit, then settle into silence again. For a time I even closed my eyes and dozed off. When I woke, he was smiling down at me. My lips echoed his smile without my volition. But I felt it. I felt like my whole body was smiling. I raised my face and kissed him.

He liked it, I could tell. But I was surprised when he pulled back, holding my face gently with both hands so I couldn't pursue him as I wanted to. I looked at him with wordless questions. No one had ever turned me back before. Especially no one I had truly wanted. It stung. Insecurities plagued me, and I couldn't fight them down this time. Tears pooled in my eyes, and I moved away on the bench, turning my face from him.

"I've hurt you," he said. "I'm so sorry."

"I'm only confused," I answered, struggling to control my voice. "You tell me I am the love of your life, the one you wanted to marry. You say you want to win me back. But you don't really want me."

He smiled, almost laughing out loud, but he bit his lip. "You think I don't want you? Believe me, I do." He held out a hand for mine, and I hesitated. I wanted to cut off all contact with him, to turn my back and run away. But I couldn't let him go. I was almost as addicted to him as I was to the Ambrosia now. I put my hand in his.

"But, you are too important to me to ..." he trailed off. "Emma, this is going to sound ridiculously old-fashioned, but I plan on waiting till marriage. I've seen enough perfectly good relationships ruined by rushing into sex. I would never want to cheapen what we have by pushing you too far."

"You do know what my job is, right?" I said through my teeth, resisting the urge to pull my hand away again.

"Of course I do," he said, and the not-quite-hidden haunting note in his voice banished my ire. "Of course. But things can change." He reached out his free hand and stroked my cheek.

I didn't know about that. But I wished it was true.

"So, you're an abstainer, are you?" I said with a sigh.

This time he did laugh. "For now, but I don't plan on staying that way. I plan on enjoying it—with you—someday."

"You mean if I marry you?" I asked, and goosebumps prickled on my skin.

"Well, yes. If you'll have me, and I mean *just* me—I couldn't take that rejection again, Emma. I couldn't." He implored me with his eyes.

"I'm not ready for that, Cale," I said gently. "Not yet."

He looked down at his knees. "But you haven't said no."

"No, I haven't," I said slowly, wishing I could find among my feelings some shred of certainty that could make me let go of my whole world. "Please," I whispered. "Please keep trying."

He closed the distance between us on the bench and put his arm around my shoulders again as my tears welled silently.

I had the feeling that he was crying, too, but acknowledging his tears would reveal mine. When I finally had myself under control again, I spoke.

"You said we were—hypothetically—engaged?"

"Mmm hmm."

"And you plan on waiting till marriage?"

"Yep."

"Then you and I—hypothetically—never ..."

"Nope."

"And you still came back for me ..." I whispered, amazed.

He didn't answer, knowing I didn't mean it as a question. He only squeezed me gently and stroked the tears from my cheek.

"I guess there *is* more to love than just sex," I said with a little, light laugh. I knew plenty about the one thing, but I was discovering I was just a baby when it came to the other.

We sat together until morning, and he put his jacket around my shoulders when I got cold. It was with a heavy heart that we watched the sun rise together. I would have stayed with him forever if I could, but the pull of the Ambrosia was too great.

"I have to get back," I murmured, reluctantly pulling away from his warmth.

"Couldn't I just pay you more to stay?" he murmured back. "In fact, how much would it take to buy you?"

"I have to get back," I repeated more emphatically, and laughed lightly, standing up slowly. But I didn't feel light. I knew Cale wasn't joking. And I might have taken him up on his offer, if things had been different. If it weren't for the Ambrosia. I was already feeling the need.

"If the time comes," I added, "There won't be money involved."

"No, there won't," Cale said, his voice and expression reflecting the sober tenor of his words. His hand appeared between us, and I looked down in confusion. When I saw the roll of money, I understood. His payment for our night together. This morning I almost felt bad taking it. Could I even offer him any part of what he wanted? Wasn't I just wasting his time?

The funny thing was I realized that I had spent the entire night beside him without asking for, or even thinking about, the money. Another first. This man was making everything new in my life. Maybe there was hope.

—

I was very pleased with myself when Sloane took me back to the warehouse that morning and gave my big fat roll of bills to Lucas. Happy, too, that I had managed to spend the entire night with Cale, and no other man. Perhaps I felt guilty for the happiness. That might have been the reason I walked away from Lucas's desk with a strange pang of dread, like I might get caught. The fact that I had technically done nothing wrong didn't assuage my newly awakened conscience.

"What is this?" Lucas' shocked, angry voice surprised me. I whirled back toward his heavy wooden desk.

"What is what?" I said, blinking. He had risen from his seat in anger—something I'd never seen him do before, even when he was berating his incompetent lackeys. He was holding out the stack of money I'd just given him. I could only assume he meant that, though I didn't understand what fault he could find with my generous earnings. "It's my take from tonight."

"Who gave it to you?" he leaned menacingly over the desk, and I was honestly frightened.

"A customer," I answered, no trace of flippancy left in my voice. I shrank back, and caught Sloane's curious, concerned eyes trained on me.

"Who?" Lucas insisted. "Who was the customer?"

I felt a large hand on my shoulder. I didn't have to turn to know it belonged to one of Lucas's massive enforcers. This was not good. But I had absolutely no clue why.

I looked from Sloane to Lucas, hesitating. "I ..." I began, planning to deny I knew Cale's name.

"Man by the name of Kynsey," Sloane said quickly, putting himself between me and Lucas, whose menacing glare was terrifying. For the first time, I could understand how Cale could consider him a villain. "Cale Kynsey, I believe."

"*Cale* Kynsey? Are you sure?" Lucas's face changed instantly as he came around the desk to lean closer to Sloane.

"I'm sure about the Kynsey part. But I think the first name's Cale. Yeah, yeah, I'm positive."

I shot Sloane a panicked look, but it was lost in the mayhem that was breaking loose. What had he just done?

"That confirms it, then," Lucas mused, rubbing his hand over his face. "Has he caused any problems for Emma?"

He considered me again, looking me up and down. If he saw anything puzzling, he didn't say.

"No, sir," Sloane answered. "But I did think it odd that he pays for her entire night and doesn't touch her."

Lucas let out a quick, loud laugh that echoed throughout the warehouse. Some of his thugs and the other girls joined in.

My face burned, not with shame, but with righteous indignation.

"I didn't think there was anything wrong with that," I said simply.

Lucas was in my face in a flash, clamping his hand none-too-gently around my chin. His eyes burned into mine.

"Did I ask you to speak?" he asked with a silk-smooth, steel-hard voice.

I stared back, scared silly, but not about to show him that. He released my chin and turned back to Sloane.

"See that Kynsey stays away from her," he ordered.

"Yes, sir," Sloane said, glancing at me with an expression of futility. He knew I'd be disappointed, but he had no choice. I understood.

"And if any of you girls get the idea you can lie down—or rather—stand up on the job," he chuckled at his own joke, "You can refer to Emma's example. Sloane, take Emma to her room. I plan on making her remember to whom she belongs."

—

I shivered as I paced under the streetlight, though it wasn't cold. A bone-deep chill had settled over me that I felt would never lift again. The shadows were darker than ever under my eyes. Lucas hadn't left a mark on my body—he was much too clever for that. But he had scarred me in ways that would never heal.

First, and perhaps worst of all, he had held back my dose of Ambrosia. Then he had by turns brutalized me with words, with pain, and with his body until I couldn't bear any more. I had resolved not to scream, cry, or give him any such satisfaction. But before long, the growing intensity of the Ambrosia withdrawal, coupled with his torture, loosened my tongue and I was sure all the girls in the place had heard. An effective warning.

As the day wore on, he had given me tiny doses of Ambrosia, simply to keep me from slipping into half-conscious tremors. Then hallucinations added to my torment, filled with disjointed images of twisted joy and bright pain. At last he had left me at sunset, with the sweetly whispered words: "You're mine, Emma."

As much as the day had been a personal hell, I was dreading the night even more. Cale would come, and I would have to turn him away. And then, as he watched, I would have to leave with another man, pretending I loved him instead. My own torment I could bear, but not Cale's. Not knowing I caused it.

The moment I feared arrived, and Cale's car drove up. I glanced at Sloane, who gave me a warning look.

"Let me say goodbye," I mouthed to Sloane, and he nodded.

I turned to Cale, who leaned toward me with a hopeful smile, popping open the door. He took one look at my face and jumped out of the car, circling it in a few long strides until he was at my side, his arms strong and warm and safe around me. In spite of myself, I melted against him and began to sob.

"What's wrong, Emma?" he crooned, holding my hair in a gentle handful at the back of my head. He kissed my forehead. Somehow, that was enough to calm my hysteria, and I unburdened the whole story. I felt his body stiffen as I told my sordid tale, his muscles tensing for some violent reaction.

"What I don't understand," I finished, "Is why he got so angry in the first place. All I did was give him your money, and he jumped on me, asking who gave it to me. It was just money!"

Cale looked off to the side, the muscles in his jaw working. "It was my fault," he said. "I sent him a message. I called him out, essentially."

"What did you do?" I asked incredulously.

"I put a mark that only he would understand on one of the bills. He would have known it was me right away. But I never thought that monster would do this to you."

He took my face in his hands, searching my eyes. I flinched away, ashamed of what Lucas had done to me. As if he could hear my thoughts, he took me gently by the shoulders.

"You don't even know who you are, what you're worth to me. That devil has beaten it out of you until you're just about crawling!" I gaped at the force of gentle Cale's rage. I wasn't scared, not like I'd been in the face of Lucas's anger. I was angry too.

Cale dropped one hand, reaching into his pocket and taking something out. I could see it was some sort of shiny metal oblong, like a mirror without a handle. It was bordered with chased silver designs, and slightly tarnished, as if it was very old.

"What's this?" I asked as he put it in my hand.

"Just look into it," he urged, helping me position it before my face. He let go, watching me expectantly.

I looked into the polished silver, surprised at the clarity of the reflection. I saw my face, the makeup I'd carefully applied to conceal my fear and pain, the perfectly straight, bobbed red–black hair. As I watched, something indescribable happened to my reflection. There seemed to be two other images superimposed on the real one.

The first showed me—for I knew it was me, somehow—weary and haggard, emaciated and spotted with blemishes, with straggling, greasy hair and dirt smeared on my face. The second was so much the opposite that it took me a moment to realize this was also me—but as I had never seen myself before, with long, flowing rose—gold hair crowned with a jewel of gleaming light like a star. My skin was luminous and soft, my eyes bright and kind, and my mouth smiling with the truest joy I'd ever seen.

I dropped the mirror.

Cale caught it deftly before it hit the ground, as if he had been anticipating my reaction, and put it back in his pocket. I was paralyzed, my hands still raised as they had been while still holding the mirror. Then Cale took my hands in his and held them against his chest. Warmth seeped into me.

"What *was* that?" I breathed in shock.

"It's what you might call magic."

"A magic mirror?" I half–laughed, though today I could believe it.

"It shows you who you are as others see you, who you are to yourself, and who you truly are."

"I beg your pardon?" I balked.

"It's hard to explain," he said. "But it was the only way to show you what I can't say. That's you, Emma. Not this plastic face you put on. Not the starveling waif that cowers inside you. You are that Princess. You are beautiful. That is who you are, and I love you."

"I can't *be* that ..." I shook my head wildly. "Not even for you."

"You already *are*," he insisted. He pulled me close. "There is so much more I want to show you." He leaned close so that his lips brushed my ear and I shivered as he whispered, "Come away with me."

My breath caught in a sob. "I can't."

He held me away from him, looking deeply into my eyes. "But you want to," he said softly. As usual, he wasn't asking me.

"I can't," I repeated emphatically. Sloane took a step towards us, but I glared at him. "I can't leave Lucas."

"You don't owe him anything, Emma!" Cale cried, angry.

"I know I don't," I snapped. "But I still can't go."

"Are you afraid of him? Did he threaten you?" Cale brushed my hair tenderly back from my face. "I can protect you."

"I know you can," I said through my tears. "But that's irrelevant. Please." I pleaded. "Please don't make me tell you."

"I won't," he promised. "Now, can we just go somewhere and talk? I promise I'll get you back on time." He looked at Sloane as he said this last.

"Cale," I said, stepping back. "I can't be with you. I—I'm not allowed to see you anymore."

Sloane took another step closer to me. Cale looked at my face in shock.

"Are *you* telling me to go, Emma?" he asked.

"I ..." my voice quavered.

Cale drew me back towards him, and I went willingly into his arms, breaking down publicly as I never had before.

"I understand," he said. "It's not your choice, for whatever reason. I would never cause you pain. I'll go, but I promise to watch over you, and if you ever want me, I will be there."

He bent down and kissed me. I wrapped my arms tightly about his neck. *Don't listen to me*, my heart screamed silently. *Take me away from here.* But I couldn't tell him what I most wanted to say. Then Sloane was forcing his arm between us and pushing Cale away. He pulled aside the edge of his jacket to show Cale his gun.

"Goodbye, Emma," Cale said, his eyes haunting.

I couldn't speak, but I knew he understood. He pulled his car away, stopping a block away in the shadows. I pulled my compact out of my purse, patently ignoring Sloane's concerned hovering as I willed the tears to stop and fixed my makeup. A car pulled up, and trembling, I got in. I forced a smile for the man in the driver's seat and leaned towards him as we sped away.

I didn't dare to look at Cale's car as we passed.

3

The first night after I said goodbye to Cale was the most agonizing night of my life. I felt like each successive man who drove me away stole a piece of my soul. With every tear I held back, I felt like another part of me had turned to stone. I could imagine only too well the tortured look in Cale's eyes as I drove past his car again and again. I couldn't do it another night. I couldn't.

At last I was alone in my room, with my head on my folded arms at the table. I had skipped the shower, and my breakfast sat cooling. There was no way I would face the mirror, after my strange and horrible farewell to Cale. I couldn't forget that magic mirror that he had shown me, with its three images. Could it possibly have been right? I was sure Cale had mixed up the images, and I truly was that 'starveling waif' as he put it. I certainly felt like it this morning.

I heard Sloane come in, but didn't look up. Instead, I turned my head to the wall and held out my arm for my needle. I was ashamed that this little pinprick was the only thing keeping me from Cale. The only thing shackling me to a world of agony. I had paid a staggering price for this dirty addiction.

"I'm sorry, princess," Sloane said softly. "I know you're having a hard time."

I still didn't look up. I couldn't respond to his paltry offering. There was nothing anyone could say that could make me feel better now. The Ambrosia began to seep through my veins, soothing jangling nerves as it went. But the deep, deep sorrow stayed.

"You should eat something. Take care of yourself. I'm worried about you." Sloane brushed my hair back from my forehead in a fatherly gesture, but I didn't move.

"It wasn't my fault—you know I had to tell him."

I knew, but I still couldn't bring myself to offer absolution.

"Give it time," he said as he opened the door. "You'll forget him."

Tears spilled down my face and dried there. I went on staring at nothing. I had no doubt I'd forget him, the way my memory worked. But I didn't want to.

———

The Ambrosia dreams were worse than usual today. Maybe Lucas had upped my dose. In any case, I didn't clue in at first when I woke up that I wasn't where I was supposed to be.

It took quite a while to make sense of the jumble and to rule out the scenes that weren't real. At last, I was able to focus my mind, and my bleary eyes, on a large, well-furnished room with a wall full of big windows. The strangest thing was the light in the room. It must have been about full noon, but I felt as if I had slept for days. Running my tongue around my mouth, I thought maybe I had.

The room was an intriguing mix of modern and vintage, with intricately paneled cream walls and large loft-style windows, a black crystal chandelier and carved mahogany four-post bed, and immaculately clean marble floors. There was a flat-screen TV on the wall, a chaise by the window, and a desk in the corner. I could see a few paneled doors. Two were closed, and the open one seemed to lead to a bathroom almost as big as the bedroom.

No sooner had I sat up than a pretty maid came into the room with a tray. She put it on the bed and repositioned my pillows.

"Where am I?" I asked.

She turned and left as if she hadn't heard me.

I pushed the tray out of my way and carefully slipped out of the Egyptian cotton sheets. There was a silk robe on a chair, and I put it on. The view from the windows showed a terrace, and beyond that a cityscape only visible from a penthouse apartment. The door to the terrace was locked. One of the closed doors proved to lead to a spacious closet with a mirrored vanity, and a few garments that looked like they would fit me but wouldn't be suitable outside the boudoir. The other closed door was locked, too.

Growling in frustration, I used the bathroom and picked at my breakfast. I'd much rather have picked up a chair and thrown it through one of the big windows, but I probably would have ended up hurting myself in the process. I had a quick shower and put on the first thing I found in the closet, tying the robe back on for as much coverage as I could get. I didn't bother with the makeup or hair styling accessories I found.

After that, I sat in the chaise and stared out the window, seeing nothing. Or rather, I was seeing rapidly flashing images, like flipping through a stack of polaroids—Cale as he looked when I first met him, the diner where we'd had our coffee, Lucas admiring the new black gown, bare feet on moonlit grass, the view from the park, me kissing Cale, Lucas in my room again, the three images of me in the mirror, Cale's face when I said goodbye, Cale kissing me ...

I would go crazy like this, if I let myself. I shook away the images, though they seemed to run in a never-ending flow in the background of my mind. Instead, I tried to focus on what came next. There was only one place I could be, I decided—only one person rich enough to own a place like this and capable of getting me here.

The door opened, confirming my suspicions. Lucas Fulbright stood there, handsome and looking like he was made of money, smiling at me in approval. I glanced only long enough to know it was him, and I turned coldly back to the window.

"Ah, you look as though you belong here, my Emma," he said in a cheerful voice, ignoring my iciness. He crossed the room with hands lifted out. I could hear the way he put a slight stress on 'my' and I didn't like it. I didn't want to be his. But I needed the Ambrosia too much to deny it. He held out his hands to take my face in his, but I flinched away, closing my eyes.

I didn't resist when he made a second attempt. I knew it was dangerous to defy him too much. He liked a bit of spirit in a woman, but I could only go so far.

"Sloane informed me that you were having a hard time," he said in a voice meant to be soothing. I had no doubt it might soothe under the right circumstances. "That Kynsey fellow has been hounding you again. Well, you needn't worry about that. You're safe here. I must apologize," he added, sitting down on the chaise with me. My muscles tensed automatically to pull my body away from his touch. "I realize I haven't been paying you the attention you deserve. Allow me to show you my concern." He caressed my face with one hand and combed his fingers through my hair.

I kept my eyes closed, refusing to respond to his touch, not even pretending. All I could see was Cale. I had sent him away. And now I could never have him back. He could never find me here. A wave of panic washed over me as Lucas kissed me. I couldn't help but stiffen, and he felt it. He stopped, mid-kiss, and leaned back, clamping his fingers around my chin. My eyes flew open reflexively in shocked fear.

"You're lucky I'm not in the mood," he said evenly, his intense eyes inches from mine. "But I will be back later. Please me, and I may make some concessions for your stay here. But if you displease me ..." he let the threat go unsaid. I knew well enough what could happen. And here, with no clients to look perfect for, it wouldn't matter how much he marked me.

He left me then, and only then did I let out my breath in a jagged sob. I looked out the window again, scanning the city as if by some miracle I could find Cale among the millions and draw him to me.

—

I turned on the TV and let the mindless drone of it pacify me through the long day. Lunch came and went, a meal I didn't often get, and then dinner. I began to get jittery as I felt the lack of Ambrosia. Lucas must have allowed me a hefty dose that last morning, when I'd been moved from the warehouse. It would have lasted a long time. But not forever. If only it could, I wouldn't be in this mess now.

He was waiting, I knew. Waiting for the tears, for the trembling, for the pleading. He would have me at his mercy,

ERIN E. M. HATTON

then, and I would do anything for him. My eyes began to rove around the room, spotting a discreet video camera in the corner. So he was watching me. He would be coming soon, when he saw that I was needing the drug.

I got up and wandered around, so far from my earlier catatonic state. I wanted to crash through the window and fly away to Cale. More than that, I wanted to break down the door and find a needle. But I wasn't ready to beg, not from that monster.

I watched the sun go down, and the lights come on in the streets like stars. There were no stars here, occluded by the haze of artificially lit fog. I leaned my forehead against the cool window, pressing my shaking, sweating palms against the glass. Pain began to prickle in my extremities, creeping inward until it felt like my limbs were on fire. I turned to the bed and lay down, curling in a ball, beginning to wonder if he would come at all. What if he wanted to punish me?

Then I began to call out. I couldn't help it.

"Please," I shouted. "Please just give it to me! I promise I'll be good."

The shouting died out into whimpers, and then tears, and then there was a voice in my ear, whispering oh so sweetly.

"It's alright, my Emma," Lucas said. "I'm here." And a flood of cool sweet release flowed into my veins, even as I despised myself for wanting it so much. Lucas began to kiss the back of my neck, and I turned to him in shameful gratitude.

—

It was a full week before I was allowed the run of the penthouse. Even then, there were locked rooms I wasn't permitted to access, no phones—though how he thought I was supposed

50

to contact anyone, I don't know—and two of his thugs guarded the door at all times. I even tried coming out of my room at night once, and I saw them there, alert as ever. I explained my untimely emergence as a craving for a midnight snack, and was sent back to my room to wait on the seemingly mute maid. For all I knew she *was* a deaf–mute. It would fit Lucas's personality to do that.

After a month of this opulent, purposeless existence, Lucas let me out on a day pass.

I found out in the morning, when I came out of the shower to find a large, red–ribboned box on the bed. I didn't care much for Lucas's presents, but as bored as I was I wouldn't ignore it. I flipped open the lid casually and appraised the contents. Heavy burgundy silk–not the bedroom variety. And lots of it. That meant going out of the apartment, likely to some fancy soiree.

I didn't relish the idea of appearing in public on Lucas's arm, trying to look happy when I was dead inside. But I did like the thought of getting out of this pretty prison. A step into the real world was a step closer to Cale. My heart quickened at the thought.

My maid's behaviour confirmed my suspicions as she bundled me back into the tub for a long soak in scented oil. She must have been instructed to prepare me for something special, for she scoured my body, went at my feet mercilessly with a pumice stone, and otherwise groomed me to death while I languished in the tub. I thanked her as I emerged, but as usual, she said nothing.

The toilette continued with waxes and lotions, creams, oils, and polishes, until I gleamed with a soft, pearl glow from head to toe. Next, she made up my face with expensive cosmetics and did my hair in a posh up–do, Audrey Hepburn style. *Where did Lucas get this woman?* I wondered. He probably paid a fortune for her, and only for serving me. If I didn't know him for the beast he was, I might have been wooed by this attention. As it was, I could only imagine what Cale would think of me, all dolled up like a princess.

Thinking that word was a mistake. Tears welled up in my eyes and I fought them down. It wouldn't do to ruin the makeup job. But it was no use. All I could think about was the last night I had seen Cale, when he had shown me his magic mirror. Looking at my reflection in the vanity mirror, I silently wept. I looked beautiful to the outward eye. But what would I look like to Cale now? Inside, I felt the wretched creature I had seen. Surely he must see that, if he were to see me now.

The maid stopped working, laying down her comb.

"I'm sorry," I muttered, trying in vain to stop the tears from spoiling her masterpiece.

To my surprise, she reached down and wrapped her arms around my shoulders, laying her cheek against mine and her cool hand on my forehead. She made a soft, voiceless, shushing noise that I found strangely soothing. Before long, the tears stopped. The maid left the room, returning in a moment with a hot washcloth. She smiled at me sympathetically in the mirror before she washed away the ruined makeup and started again.

—

I tried to appear calm, as though anything in my world was normal, when Lucas came to collect me. I was just getting my earrings put on—diamond and jet affairs that likely cost more than I did. The dress was stunning, something I would have died for in my self-absorbed days before Cale had turned my life upside-down, burgundy and black shot silk, strapless, with a full tucked and trailing skirt that floated around me. The whole thing was laced with subtle embroidery and scattered with random crystals that caught the light like tiny stars. I had never felt so beautiful—and so ugly—in all my life.

I took Lucas's arm woodenly, remembering involuntarily how Cale had offered his arm the same way on our first 'date' together. I felt a wave of shame as I recalled how he had paid for my time. Now, after everything I'd put him through, I would have gladly given him every moment left to me, asking nothing in return.

Lucas escorted me down to a waiting limo, smiling as he handed me into the car like we were a happy couple. It reminded me in a sick, twisted way of the natural couple-like gestures Cale and I had shared—holding hands, a touch at the small of my back, resting my head on his shoulder, a light kiss. Sharing those same things with Lucas now felt cheap and disgusting, like a mockery of the sweet, fledgling intimacy I had begun with Cale.

"Congratulations, Emma," Lucas said as he slid into the limo next to me. "You've earned this freedom tonight. And I must say, you will do nicely as my date this evening. I should have thought of this a long time ago. You look the part quite well." I accepted his kiss unenthusiastically, but didn't resist. He was ebullient enough not to notice, and he poured a glass of champagne for both of us.

"To you, my Emma," he toasted, looking at me over the rim of his glass. I hated more than anything his insistence on calling me *his*. Hated, hated, hated it.

"You are a very lucky girl, you know," he said, putting an arm around my shoulders and watching the streetscape slide by the dark tinted window. "This is the social event of the year. I disappointed many beautiful young ladies by bringing you."

"I'm honoured," I said, reserving my biting sarcasm for my private indulgence.

"Yes, you should be. The crème–de–la–crème will be there tonight. You could get for yourself an enviable position if tonight goes well." The implied threat in his words spoke louder than the promise of reward. He was preaching to the choir, though. I knew better than to misbehave.

As the limo slowed at a crowded red carpet, I took on a persona like an actress. I knew how to do this, and although this wasn't quite the role I was used to playing, I knew how to make people like me. I put on my smile like an accessory as the door opened, and I followed Lucas out of the limo.

Flashes burned my retinas, but I ignored them from within my happy façade. I could only imagine the pictures in the society pages and gossip tabloids. It ripped out my heart to think what Cale would see if he were to glimpse one of these photos on a newsstand somewhere. Would he see past the exterior to the frightened caged bird that flailed within me? Or would he see only as the rest of the world—the confident, smiling woman, dressed like a queen, leaning adoringly toward his archenemy. I was beginning to understand the effects of the betrayal I had once caused him, if his fantastic, tragic story was true. But I was far from comprehending what could lead me to do such a thing in the first place.

Lucas led me into the lobby of a fine hotel, and beyond

to a spacious ballroom. The place was already crowded with well-dressed, wealthy-looking people. Perhaps not every eye turned to look at us, but it felt like nine pairs out of ten followed us into the room. The flow of the crowd shifted, and I felt them begin to jockey for position to speak with the powerful Lucas Fulbright and meet his lovely new escort.

I spoke as graciously as I could muster to everyone who addressed me, though I wanted to curl up in the fetal position and scream. "How did you meet Mr. Fulbright?" they all wanted to know. "Where do you come from?" "Who are your people?" "Where did you get your gown?" Lucas answered for me as much as possible, but soon I began to learn his story and perpetuate his lie. After all, what was I supposed to say? Until very recently I was a prostitute in Mr. Fulbright's employ, until he beat me, drugged me, and dragged me off as his prisoner, among other things.

I wanted to run out into the street and shout at the top of my lungs for Cale to come and get me. I wanted to shoot up a good healthy dose of Ambrosia and blot out the milling, noisy, interrogating crowd. But as I could do neither, I retreated further and further into myself until I felt like a passenger inside a woman-shaped robot. An attractive, charming woman, but not me.

Perhaps it was my longing for Cale that conjured up a hallucination, but something definitely caught my notice, bringing my withdrawn self back into my present surroundings. Thankfully I had not been speaking at the time, or I would have made a fool of myself by stopping mid-sentence. I doubted I could have recovered gracefully from this shock.

Across the ballroom, I could swear I had seen him—yes,

it had to be. He was standing in the midst of a mob of people, dressed impeccably in a tux. But his eyes were trained on me. My heart, which I'm not even sure had been beating previously, lurched into motion like the rumble of a sports car in a pursuit.

I knew I had to see him. No matter what the risk, I had to try. It was likely the only chance I'd ever get to tell him all the things I wanted to say.

"Excuse me, Lucas," I practically purred, rubbing my hand on his shoulder as I smiled up at him. "I have to use the ladies' room."

He looked at me with a touch of suspicion in his eyes, but he dared not insist on coming with me in front of our latest companions. He smiled back affably and said, "Don't be too long." Others would hear only the desire of a man for the company of his lover. But I knew it was a warning, and only that.

I smiled and nodded, and glided off in the direction of the restrooms. I cast a negligent glance in Cale's direction, so not to draw undue attention to him, and saw that he mirrored my movements from the other side of the room. It took all of my power not to break into a run, but thankfully the thought of broken neck by high heels helped to keep me walking at a normal pace. By the time I reached the restroom doors, my heart was hammering, and my breath came ragged. I was sure everyone could see the red flush of fear and excitement on my cheeks.

I looked from side to side, looking for Cale, looking for observers. Someone in a tux passed near to me, and though I only saw him in my peripheral vision, I thought it to be Cale.

A waft of air from his passage came over me, and I knew him for certain by his scent. I caught my breath, as though determined to hold in as much of him as I could. I turned slightly, and saw his figure disappear through a service door out of the corner of my eye.

I waited for an intolerably long moment, counting the seconds and observing the people in the lobby. At last, it seemed no one was watching me. I slipped quietly through the service door and into a narrow corridor. I hadn't gone far when a hand reached out and pulled me into another doorway. Stifling a shriek of surprise, I followed. The door closed on a small linen room, and I was enveloped in a fervent embrace.

I reached up and held onto his lapels, burrowing my face into his starched white shirt and weeping. I could feel his lips in my hair, and his ragged breath as he wept too. His arms held me so tightly I could hardly breathe, but I wanted him to hold me tighter still, so that I could be sure no one would ever be able to tear me away again. After a long moment simply holding and weeping, he took my face with his hands and kissed me.

"Cale," I said brokenly. It was all I could say.

"I know," he whispered. "I know."

"I'm sorry. I'm so, so sorry."

"Shh. It'll be alright. Don't cry, my Emma." Now that sounded right. I was *his* Emma—I always had been.

"I don't know what to do!" I sobbed. "I can't go back to him, I can't. I want to be with you so badly."

"But?" Cale asked, anticipating my next words. I took a deep breath, ready to tell him the dark secret I'd never shared with anyone.

"But...Cale, there's this drug. I can't...I can't live without it."

I felt a rumble like a silent snarl building in his chest. "So this is how he does it—how he keeps you prisoner."

I laid my head on his chest and wept with the futility of it all. "I shouldn't have come," I cried. "Now I'll go back to him and it'll be worse than ever when he sees I've been crying. I think he would kill you if he got the chance."

"Don't worry about me," Cale growled. "I wish I had known that this was the reason...before, when you told me to leave."

"I don't see how it could have made any difference."

"It makes every difference in the world." He took my face in his hands and captivated me with his eyes. "Emma, my love can overcome anything. I would go to the grave and back for you. Do you believe that?"

"Yes," I whispered, feeling goosebumps rise on my bare arms and shoulders.

"Then trust me," he said, looking into my eyes as though the sheer force of his gaze could impress this truth on me. "Come with me."

"Okay," my mouth said. I had thought my heart was racing before. Now it kicked into overdrive, reminding me of the danger that waited if I crossed Lucas. But it was too late. I wanted Cale more than the Ambrosia now, I knew it.

The word was all Cale needed, and he took my hand. Propping open the door, he scouted the corridor, then pulled me after him. Rather than heading back to the crowded lobby, he took me back through the service section of the hotel. I wondered if he had planned this in advance, or if he was just this good at finding his way out of a predicament. I didn't care, as long as we got out unscathed.

We emerged in a parking garage, and Cale's grey car was waiting by the door. Planned, then, I guessed. Cale helped me into the back seat, following me in. I noticed then that another man sat in the driver's seat, and a second rode shotgun.

"Go, Mike," he said urgently. "Lay down on the floor," he added to me, gently helping me down as the car rolled into motion and covering me with the garment bag that hung from the back window. His hand reached casually under the nylon bag and rested comfortingly and possessively on my head. It felt good, and right.

After a long time driving, I was just beginning to cramp up when Cale patted me on the shoulder.

"You can get up now," he said. "It's safe."

I looked around, blinking at the lights. We were in an unfamiliar area of the city—neither posh enough to be Lucas's home ground, nor seedy enough to be mine. Safe enough, then, though I still feared I would never be free from Lucas. I climbed up onto the seat, smoothing back my hair and adjusting my dress.

Cale held out an arm for me to rest within, and I leaned gratefully against his chest. He had loosened his tie and undone his top button, and with his hair mussed by the nervous roving of his hand, he had an endearing rakish quality. I could see his reflection in the side mirror of the car, and even that likeness showed me the ravages of the past month. His eyes were sunken with dark circles, and deep lines etched around his mouth and across his forehead.

What had he endured for the long days and weeks not knowing where I was, or if I was even alive? I lifted my head to study his face. He felt my gaze and looked back at me with a questioning smile. I tried to smile back, but the tears came afresh.

"I'm sorry," I whispered, raising a hand to cup his face. "I'm so sorry."

"It doesn't matter now," he answered, and he captured my hand and kissed it. I noticed then a fierce flicker of hope in his eyes. Whatever damage I had done to him, it could be repaired with love. He gathered me close to his chest again.

We watched the city go by, in an oasis of companionable silence, both afraid to speak of the hell we faced. The motion of the car lulled me with a peace I hadn't felt in a long time. Before long, we turned into an underground parking garage. Cale lifted me out of the car.

"I can walk," I murmured, trying to right myself.

"Let me," he insisted. I laid my head willingly back against his solid shoulder, clinging to the cloak of peace a while longer. After all, I wasn't really sure I could stand, now that the adrenaline was wearing off. I was aware of his two friends who fell into step with Cale—a tall, broadly built brown-haired one in front, and a lean, quick-looking blond one behind. So, Cale had his own protectors, too. I wondered if I had known them in my forgotten days. Judging by the surreptitious, curious glances they kept giving me, I guessed I had.

They took me into the elevator, where Cale still refused to put me on my feet. The walls were mirrored, and I glimpsed our reflection. I liked the way we looked together, with his strong arms carrying me, and the tender, introspective look in his eyes that he didn't realize I could see.

We got off at the seventh floor and went halfway down the hall. The big man, whom Cale had called Mike, opened the door, looking both ways inside, before he let Cale in with a nod. They weren't taking any chances.

The apartment was a modest, middle–class type of place, but it felt more comfortable than Lucas's palatial penthouse. There were a couple of couches in the living room, both strewn with blankets in a way that suggested Cale's two friends had taken up residence there. The kitchen was bright and relatively clean, with a few dishes piled by the sink. Down the hall I saw a bathroom and two bedrooms.

The blond man moved the blankets out of the way and made a show of dusting off the cushions before Cale put me down. A pillow appeared at my back and a blanket over my legs, and I sank into place gratefully.

"Are you alright?" Cale asked. The man named Mike held out a glass of water, and I took a sip. I nodded.

"I'm fine. A little scared," I admitted.

"Don't worry," Cale kissed my forehead. "I'm here." He sat down beside me and moved my head into his lap. "Emma, these are my friends, Mike and Gabe."

"Hi," I said, feeling a little awkward lying down, but under the circumstances I thought I could be forgiven.

"Hey," said Mike with a quick nod.

"Good to have you back," Gabe said with a smile. The way they looked at me confirmed that they knew me from before. I wondered what they thought of my return. Did they support Cale's rescue wholeheartedly? Or did they think it was a mistake to pursue me and that their friend could do better? It didn't help to know in my heart that he really could do better than me.

"So we've got a limited time before ..." Cale trailed off, and I knew he meant the Ambrosia. My heart sank. I hadn't forgotten about that part, in the excitement, but I'd at least put off thinking about it. I wanted to share Cale's hope that I could make it through. But remembering those few times when I had experienced a taste of withdrawal, I was afraid of what I might face.

"Yeah," I said. Sensing the apprehension in my voice, Cale squeezed my hand reassuringly.

"Maybe you should eat something."

"Is there anything I can change into, first?" I asked tentatively.

Cale laughed a little. "Yeah, I guess you don't want to sit around in that dress, do you? It's pretty on you, though," he added with a smile that made me blush. That was another new thing for me—blushing.

He helped me to my feet again and took me down the hall to a bedroom. Opening a drawer, he revealed a few things he had bought for me to wear.

"You were planning on abducting me?" I asked, an eyebrow raised at him.

"Hoping to, anyway," he said with a shrug.

"At least you thought this out, because if it was up to me, I would have ended up in this ball gown forever." I laughed, then sobered under his steady gaze. "Thank you."

His eyes filled with all the gratitude, hope and pure, ridiculous love he felt for me. Then he backed out of the room and shut the door.

I peeled quickly out of the burgundy dress, letting it pool on the floor and kicking it viciously into the corner. The earrings followed. I was suddenly eager to rid myself of every touch Lucas had left on me. Grabbing a large towel from the back of the door, I slipped out of the room and into the shower. I scrubbed as I never had before, not stopping until all the makeup, hairspray, and scented oil was gone down the drain.

Feeling somewhat better now, I wrapped myself securely in my towel and scurried back to the bedroom. I mused over the clothes in the drawer—a few pairs of jeans, some yoga pants, and a selection of long and short-sleeved shirts ranging from the kind of thing you'd wear out on an informal date to workout wear. I rested my hands on the edge of the drawer for a minute, stopping to look at my scoured face in the little mirror that rested on the dresser's top.

What came next? A life with Cale? I hoped so, I really did. But I knew what came before that—between this moment and forever. First, there was the monster of the Ambrosia to deal with. I shuddered at the thought, as unbidden memories of tremors and fiery pain and sweat and vomit came to my mind. Could I make it through? Could Cale still love me at the end of it?

Gritting my teeth, I combed my wet hair carefully behind my ears. I reached for the yoga pants and t-shirt. They'd probably have to go in the garbage when this was over.

With a deep breath, I opened the door to my room. Three pairs of eyes looked up when I came in, as though surprised in the middle of a deep discussion. Cale said something in a low voice to his companions, effectively ending their conversation. Mike and Gabe got up and went into the kitchen—Gabe to wash dishes, and Mike to turn on the stove.

Cale smiled dazzlingly at me as he rose from the couch, taking my hand and pulling me to him. He kissed me softly.

"Feel better?" he asked as we sat down together.

"A little," I said. I did. Being with Cale made anything better, and I began to feel foolish for doubting his love.

"Mike's getting you something to eat. Hey, Mike, better keep it something light!" he shouted in the direction of the kitchen.

"I was thinking soup," the big man replied.

"Sounds good," Cale affirmed. I realized they were drawing the same conclusion that I had when choosing my clothes. This could get messy.

I ate my soup gratefully, since it had been a while since I'd had anything to eat. I hadn't been at the ball long enough to eat anything, and I'd had been far too tied up in knots anyway. Cale stroked my hair rhythmically, soothing me. Gabe collected my bowl, and I could tell he was checking to see how I was doing. Mike sat down on the other couch and put on the TV.

I laid my head down on Cale's shoulder, and felt the first twinges of longing. *Here we go*, I thought. But I wasn't going to say anything yet. I couldn't bear the concerned looks everyone was casting in my direction. I would stay strong as long as I could, keeping silent until I couldn't hold it in anymore.

The jangling followed the longing, making my limbs restless. But I forced myself to stay still on the couch. My eyes roved this way and that, unable to focus on the TV. Cale's hand landed warmly on mine, and I realized I had been twisting my fingers together violently. I looked up sharply to see his warm eyes watching me.

"You don't have to pretend it's okay, Emma," he whispered. The self-preservation instinct was so strong that I almost denied it. But whether it was the build-up of stress combined with my vulnerable position, or simply the safe feeling of Cale's presence, I cracked, and began to weep. He held my head against him. I didn't feel any better, but I felt like I might actually be able to face this beast.

After a bit, I needed to get up and walk around. I looked out the window for a while, not at the brilliant, vast cityscape of Lucas's penthouse vista, but at a hemmed-in courtyard with a children's playground lit by a couple of inadequate streetlights. When I turned back into the room, I noticed Mike and Gabe had made themselves scarce. I was thankful for that blessing—now the only audience I had for my crash-and-burn was Cale.

He was still sitting on the couch, understanding that I needed some space right now. But his eyes followed my restless roving everywhere I went. With a weak smile that I didn't feel, I went into the kitchen. I put away all the dishes Gabe had washed, probably in the wrong places, then I took the broom from its place between the fridge and the wall and swept up a few crumbs from the floor. It was pointless really, didn't need to be done, but I needed something to occupy me until the agony got to be too much.

That time was swift in coming, and I grabbed the corner of the counter with a gasp at the shooting pain in my legs. Cale was behind me in an instant, bearing me up when my legs buckled. He turned me in his arms and picked me up. I was too far gone to protest now, but drew my breath in sharply at a fresh onslaught of pain as he carried me to the bed.

He laid me down and smoothed my hair back from my face. I curled up in anguish, turning away from those haunted eyes. Every time I gasped, he flinched. When I called out for Lucas to give me the drug, he patiently reminded me: "I'm here. It's me, Cale." When I lost my soup, he had a bowl there for me. He whispered in my ear and stroked my hair. I hated that I was dragging him through this pain with me. But I didn't have the capacity, or the courage, to send him away.

Time stretched to a standstill, so that there were no more increments. It seemed to quicken and slow like waves, with each flash of pain that wracked me. I had experienced this part before, though rarely. And there had always been the hope that a fix would come to make it go away in the end.

Sometime in the interminable hours when I lay shaking in Cale's arms, I passed the threshold of known territory. After that, everything was a new torture. I began to see disjointed images, flashing incoherently through my mind. Voices echoed in the room—some angry, some tender. I felt sweet caresses and brutal blows. As the hallucinations became sharper, the apartment room, the bed, the dripping faucet in the bathroom, Cale's strong arms around me and his wordless whispering in my ear faded away.

The dreams became my reality ...

4

Air filled my lungs, life creeping with gentle tendrils through my body, quickening me.

I opened my eyes to a brilliant light that should have been blinding, but was only beautiful. Dazzling, white–gold and dancing so thickly around me that I thought I could reach out and touch it. I could see the fluttering gold–green shapes of leaves and bobbing globes of shiny fruit on slender branches waving above me. My head was pillowed on soft and fragrant moss that stretched in undulating mounds in the hollow where I lay, dotted with small white flowers.

The sun warmed my skin, glowing on my cheekbones. The breeze cooled me, whispering past my ears and lifting my hair in strands. Along with the wind came the noises of birds and animals, and distant music. And a voice, very nearby.

"My love," it whispered, and the breeze was a breath. I turned in wonder to meet a pair of grey–green eyes. They belonged to a princely man who knelt beside me. He was dressed in robes of white that seemed to shine with reflected light. As I took him in, I realized the light wasn't merely reflected. It *came* from him. There was a kind of crown around his brow that shone as though the jewel set in the centre was a star.

When I saw him, my heart leaped and raced like a deer. I smiled in amazement as he laced his fingers with mine.

"Kaehl," I voiced the name my heart supplied.

"Immah," he whispered, kissing my brow. "My Immah."

That was my first memory, and the moment I first met my beloved.

—

Writhing on the bed, my pain refined and sharpened my vision. Simultaneously I was in the gloom, hemmed in by four walls and the unrelenting love of Cale's embrace and in the gorgeous, unearthly colour and light of that other world that I used to know, long ago, somehow. I didn't understand how it could be—how I could have existed in a time and place apart, nor how I could have forgotten it so completely. I only accepted it as true. More true, perhaps, than anything else I had known before.

It was like a dream—this other place more beautiful than anything my imagination could conjure. Only in a dream could everything be so perfect, the colours so pure, the love so sweet without trace of bitterness. Except that calling it a dream didn't seem quite right. Lying there in agony, I felt that the other reality of my memories seemed like real life, the way it should be. This dark, brutish world was the dream—a nightmare from which I'd always hoped I would awaken.

I gasped as lightning—hot pain shot up my legs and squeezed my brain. Cale's hand gripped me, a solid handhold in a maelstrom of chaos. I gripped back.

"What is it? What is that place?" I managed to ask.

"It's Otherworld," he said. "Our home."

—

The day Kaehl made me, he brought me home in front of him on the back of his white horse. We made a progress across a verdant valley he called Parras. People lined our path, making a colourful avenue that led to a glowing white palace. The gates stood open to us in welcome. The air was filled with music and cheering.

I turned to Kaehl in wonder.

"What is all this?"

"They want to welcome you," he said, touching my cheek lightly with his fingertip. "They are happy to see me pleased. They know how long I have waited for you."

I beamed under his regard. I could easily understand how the people would want to see their Prince pleased.

Dismounting beneath the great arching gateway, he took me by the hand and led me into the palace of Naeve, the home he'd built for me before I'd even existed. There were courtyards filled with statues and elaborate tracery, lush, fragrant cool gardens, quiet chambers with painted walls and luxurious cushions, and vast grand halls that echoed with reverent whispers and the soft music of fountains.

At last we came into the throne room, a long, vaulted chamber lined with galleries bursting with people and festooned with banners. Kaehl led me to a dais, where two thrones awaited.

"Here is your Princess," he called to the onlookers.

They shouted their acclaim and I stood before them, wide-eyed and grateful.

—

Princess. The word rolled around in my tortured brain like a marble. It was Sloane's pet name for me, I remembered. How ironic. What kind of princess was I, lying here in this tiny bedroom, covered in my own puke and sweat, held in the arms of the prince I'd betrayed?

The question remained: if that was truly the life I'd lived, why in heaven and earth would I have thrown it away for this?

—

"Tell me again," I coaxed Kaehl. "Tell me how I came to be."

"I told you," he said, smiling. He didn't mind sharing this story, no matter how many times he told it. He touched my face, and the wind stirred my long, red–gold tresses and the skirts of my white dress.

"I never tire of hearing it."

"I was lonely," he said. He drew me into his embrace. "I wanted someone to love, someone to share all this with." He swept his eyes up to the perfect blue sky and across the mountain meadow where we sat. "So I fashioned your hair from the beams of the setting sun," and he loosened a strand of my hair from the rest, following it to the end and letting it fall, "your eyes from the autumn sky," he brushed his thumbs over my eyelids and kissed them, "your skin from the winter snow," his fingers traced over my cheeks and my eyes remained closed, "your lips from the rose," he kissed my parted lips lightly, "and your voice from the lark." His fingers came to rest lightly on my throat.

"You know the rest," he whispered in my ear.

I caught my breath and leaned against him. "When will we marry?" I asked, for the thousandth time. My hand covered the interlaced ring that circled my finger and held it against my heart.

"When the time is right," he replied for the thousandth time. When he glanced at my expression, he smiled and laid his hand along my face. "Soon."

I picked up a small fruit from the basket we'd brought

with us, and put it in his mouth. He returned the favour with a smile. He loved to share things with me.

Too soon the sun was sinking low over the green oval bowl of the valley of Parras, turning the walls of the distant white palace of Naeve into pale iridescent shell. I sighed, knowing our time alone was over. Kaehl kissed my ear and rose, stowing the food in his saddlebags. He held out his hand to me, raising me to my feet and lifting me to the back of his white horse. He mounted behind me and settled me safely in his arms before he spurred toward home.

Mikaehl was waiting for us at the palace gates with his own horse, and I could feel Kaehl tense behind me when he saw him. It was trouble, I knew, and I was concerned. I had not been a part of the world for long, but I knew there was something brewing that had Kaehl preoccupied. No one would tell me what the problem was, and I had given up asking, for now.

I knew before a word was spoken that I would be alone tonight. Gavreyl came out of the gates in haste and helped me down from the horse. I turned my eyes back to Kaehl in entreaty, but I knew better than to hope that he would stay. He was the Prince, and he must go. He leaned down to kiss me, and then he wheeled his horse away toward the horizon, followed at a swift gallop by his Champion and his best warriors.

"Come inside, Princess," Gavreyl said, motioning for me to precede him. "It's not safe out here."

With a backward glance for my beloved, the star flashing from his brow as he rode away, I passed through the gates.

—

Alone in my room, I removed the shining, star–set circlet that was my right as Kaehl's intended bride and his vice-regent, and laid it on its stand. Syrah, Davorah and Annayeh, my three ladies-in-waiting and my dearest friends, attended me, one brushing out my loose waves, one unlacing my white gown, and the third washing my feet in a basin of hot water strewn with rose petals.

My chambers were beautiful. Kaehl had designed this place perfectly for me. My audience chamber was a rotunda, with a domed roof of white stone that was carved intricately on every inch. Between the pillars of the wall were tapestries that showed some of our favourite scenes of Parras. Adjoining were my private rooms: my bath chamber, dressing room, and my bed chamber, my private dining room and my own bright, sunny conservatory where I might weave and paint and make music and create to my heart's content. Across from the main entrance to my chambers was a large open portal to a marble terrace and a stair that led to a private walled garden just for me.

It was everything that should have made me happy, and yet I could not free myself from worry for Kaehl.

"You seem preoccupied, Princess," Annayeh said as she dried my feet.

"I only wish I knew what was troubling Prince Kaehl," I sighed, staring at my reflection.

Syrah and Davorah exchanged glances, and I wondered how much they knew. Clearly they had been instructed not to speak of this with me.

"The Prince will reveal all to you when the time is right," Annayeh said calmly. Her tone irritated me. *When the time is right.* How I grew tired of those words!

I was restless, but didn't move as Syrah wove my hair

into a snug plait for the night. I obediently held up my hands for the white embroidered nightdress that Davorah put over my head. But though they led me to my bed and turned back the covers for me, I wouldn't sleep that night. Not with Kaehl away on some unknown errand of battle.

When my ladies were gone, I sat back up, resting my folded arms on my bent knees and my chin on my forearms. From my room I could see a view of the moonlit valley stretching down and away, with the silver river Anneyl winding a path between the feet of the mountains. I could see the verdant fields and lush orchards where the fruit was always in season. I could see the forests that mantled the mountains.

But there was one particular spot my eye always found—more and more of late—the dark pass of Rysha between the two southernmost mountains where the twisted trees of Iffreyn Wood seemed to hoard the light and stow it away from all eyes. I wondered what that place was, what it looked like up close, and where it led.

Perhaps I wouldn't have cared quite so much if Kaehl had not asked me to promise never to go there. I imagined it had something to do with his mysterious errands, since these two things were the only secrets he had ever kept from me. Everything else was mine to explore, mine to ask, save for this one place and this one question.

I sighed and flopped down on my pillow, rolling away from the window. I didn't need to look, for the image of Rysha was now ingrained in my memory. I couldn't wait long before I knew the answers.

—

Kaehl still had not returned by morning, and I ate my breakfast in uneasy solitude. I was impatient, though for what, I didn't know. There didn't seem to be much to be impatient for.

My ladies dressed me, and I went to the cavernous, gleaming white throne room to fulfil my vice-regnal duties. I had the care of petitioners when Kaehl was away. The place was milling with courtiers, gathered in knots here and there in their jewel-toned liveries, leaning on the railings of galleries to command a better view. The people hushed and bowed as I entered, sweeping across the stone floor inlaid with Kaehl's interlaced emblem. It was my right, my place, my duty. But my heart was not in it today. My eyes kept rising to the south window, where I could see the dark pass clearly framed between the pillars.

I dismissed the rest of the petitioners at noon, and took my lunch where I sat, on my ornate chair at the foot of Kaehl's mighty throne. I couldn't keep my gaze from the window, hoping to see my beloved returning. But in truth, I was thinking more of the mystery of the pass than of him right now.

I asked for my horse to be saddled before I even resolved my intentions. I was allowed to ride without Kaehl, of course. It was something I enjoyed on a regular basis. But if they had known that I might disobey Kaehl and go to the pass, they might not have let me go. So, with heart pounding and knees trembling, I rode west until the trees covered me from view, then turned my horse south.

It would have been a pleasant ride, watching the river undulate beside me and the friendly overhanging branches forming a canopy over my road. But I could think of nothing but the mystery I wished so much to unravel, and thus could not enjoy anything else. I looked over my shoulder from time to time, afraid someone might be following me, but I was alone.

I reached the southern end of the valley in excellent time, and my horse was showing the consequences of my haste. As the valley floor rose up to meet the skirt of the mountains, my mount slowed, until in a clearing, she stopped altogether.

With a sigh, I dismounted, tethering her so she could graze while I continued on foot. I crossed the sunny meadow, seeing on the far side the border of the dark forest of Iffreyn I had glimpsed from the palace. I took a deep breath, trying to steady my heartbeat. I had felt excitement before—that intoxicating rush of feeling that flooded me when I was flying on horseback down a steep hillside, or wrapped in Kaehl's arms. But this exhilaration was something different and new. There was a sense of danger that made me feel almost ill. Somehow I didn't mind. I had to know the answers.

I hesitated by the edge of the trees, still on the sunny side of the shadow's sharp edge. A wind picked up, tossing the branches of dark conifers so that they looked like they were beckoning to me. Deep in the gloom the wind chased away, stirring up soft sighs and whispers as it moved the trees. *Come,* the imagined voices said. I gathered my will to cross over.

Arms wrapped around me and pulled me away.

With a cry of surprise, I whirled, coming face-to-face with my beloved. Kaehl's noble face was contorted in shocked fear as he searched mine for some trace of my reasoning.

"Why are you here?" he asked in a hushed whisper, holding my face gently in his hands. "Why did you come here, Immah?" He held me tightly against him, not roughly, but as though he was afraid to let me go. I had never seen him afraid before, and it startled me.

I tried to answer, but my voice quavered.

"It's alright," he said soothingly. "You're safe. I'm here, and you're safe."

I could sense Mikaehl's questions as we passed him. Kaehl put me up on his own horse and mounted. He motioned for Mikaehl to collect my horse, and we turned northward to the palace.

I fought the urge to look back. Now that I had seen Kaehl's reaction to my near-disobedience, I was chastened. I had no wish to disappoint or frighten my love. I would not return here, but I would solve the mystery for once and for all.

—

The evening was our favourite time of the day. When the care of the kingdom was done, before night obscured the beauty of our valley, we would find a place to be alone together. Sometimes we rode out to a mountain meadow, or a large flat rock overlooking the river, or our secret mossy clearing where we had first met. Other times we found a corner of the palace or its gardens where we might be able to talk about the day uninterrupted, enjoying the delights of the cool breeze and the sounds and scents it brought to us.

Tonight the breeze was perfumed with ripe fruit from our eastern vineyards, distinctly intoxicating as it reached us at the battlements of Naeve's single pinnacle where we looked out on the panorama of purple mountains. But something felt different tonight—a constriction in my heart that would not seem to ease.

Kaehl seemed pensive, but patient, as if he was waiting for me to broach the subject of today's events. I knew he wasn't pleased, but he was not angry. With a sigh, I spoke at last.

"I'm sorry about what happened," I said, looking down at my clasped hands where they lay on my white skirts.

Kaehl put his hand under my chin and guided my face to look at him. I wanted to flinch away, but I couldn't tear myself from the love in his eyes.

"There is nothing to forgive," he said simply, his thumb stroking my cheek. "You did not go into Iffreyn."

"No," I said. "But I was closer than you liked."

"Yes," he confirmed, his voice tight.

"Won't you tell me what it is you don't want me to see?" I tried not to sound petulant.

"Isn't it enough that I asked you to stay away, for your safety?" His voice was gentle.

I wanted to say yes, but that wouldn't be truthful. Instead of answering, I bit my lip and shrugged, letting my head fall against his shoulder.

"Immah, you may already have guessed this, for I know you are clever ..." I could feel him smile briefly as his cheek grew firm against my brow. Then his voice grew serious. "I have an Enemy."

I shivered and pulled closer to Kaehl.

"He has wronged me grievously. So great was his crime, that we do not speak his name anymore. I would let him live, alone in exile, but he will not give up. I fear he will stop at nothing to see all that I love destroyed." I looked up at him, and saw his eyes fixed in concern on the dark shadow of If-freyn on the southern mountains. He looked down at me with a smile that belied his worry. "Is that enough for you?"

I smiled back, with a nod. It was enough. Seeing the fear etched around Kaehl's eyes made me never want to go near the dark pass of Rysha and the wood of Iffreyn again.

"I should take you to your chamber, now," he said, watching the light fade from the sky.

I held to his arm, reluctant to let go.

He chuckled. "Immah, my love," he chided. "Soon we will never be apart again. But you must remember, we will always have our kingdom to care for."

"But why do we work so much for this kingdom?" I asked. "I love this land as much as you do," I added, "but you have servants who could do everything without you."

"Serving my kingdom is my privilege, my Immah," he said, turning smiling eyes out over the vast valley of Parras. I knew it was only a small part of our land, although I had not yet seen the rest. "We are a part of this kingdom, interconnected with it. Like this," he said, pointing to the knotwork emblem on his chest. "I hope that you can come to feel that way in time." He looked back to me and took my hand, brushing my knuckles against his lips. "Now, to bed, my darling."

—

I knew before I opened my eyes the next morning that Kaehl was gone from the palace. I had become so attuned to his presence, and his absence, that I could feel the subtle difference in the voices, the noises, even the atmosphere around the palace that meant the Prince was away. There was a sense—not of fear, but certainly of urgency, of tension.

I felt in no hurry to rise, but I knew I would feel better if I did. My ladies helped me dress, but understood from my pensive mood that I preferred not to talk this morning. Now that I knew a little about Kaehl's reasons for secrecy, I was worried, just as he feared I would be. The thought of him pursuing, and perhaps facing some vengeful enemy left me cold.

As I prepared to leave the room, Syrah leaned close to me, her long, brown hair brushing my shoulder.

"Don't be afraid," she said in a tender voice that softened her boldness. "Prince Kaehl is mighty, and he will prevail."

I drew myself up straighter, remembering my purpose here, and the one who loved me. She was right. Kaehl could take care of himself. He needed me to do his work here.

"Thank you," I replied, glancing at her with newly brightened eyes as I swept from the room.

As I entered the throne room, I made a point of really looking at the people there: the farmers bringing portions of their crops and livestock, the artisans with their creations, even children come to share stories with their Prince. Now that I understood how important this kingdom was to my beloved—how he preferred to serve them himself rather than delegate the work, as was his right—I saw the people differently.

They were not merely subjects—they were companions. They were not all the same, but each had a name, a face, and a story. I made an effort, more than ever before, to know each one who came in supplication. I remembered Kaehl's love for them and loved them as he did.

In the midst of the tributes and praises, the boons and the benevolence, I saw something that caught my eye. There was a man, standing in the shadowed corner, who watched the proceedings but stood aloof. He did not seem to be a petitioner, for he made no effort to approach me. By his dress, I marked him as noble, just short of princely. He wore a deep red cloak over a dark tunic, and some unfamiliar heraldry I could not make out. His head was covered with a deep hood, but when he turned to me I caught a glimpse. His hair and beard were dark, his skin pale, and his keen eyes fixed on me. I did not recognize him from Kaehl's court.

There was something about him that captured my attention, something beyond the mystery of his presence. He was watching me, which was not strange of itself. As Princess, I was used to being under constant regard. No, it was the way he watched me—the hungry way his eyes seemed to devour me. I had never seen such a thing before. Though I tried to imagine who he might be and what his business was, none of my explanations seemed enough.

After I had finished meeting with Kaehl's subjects, I looked for him, but he had vanished.

—

I took my midday meal alone in my room, preferring to be away from the crowds for a while, especially with Kaehl away. Davorah brought me my lunch and set it on the table where I could overlook the garden that Kaehl had planted for me. There was a fine breeze today, and it tossed the branches of trees and shrubs, setting the slender stalks of the flowers waving and bowing as though their Prince was walking by.

I had all but forgotten the strange nobleman from the throne room, when I caught sight of a small folded square of parchment with a deep red emblem on it, resting on the chair next to me. It was some kind of rune, but none I had ever seen before, all sharp angles and strange curves. It was nothing like Kaehl's heraldry of two intersecting lines within an interlaced circle. I picked up the parchment, curious how it had arrived here, and opened the seal.

*Princess...*it read...*I have a petition to put to you, but I fear I cannot make it in public. Please meet me in your garden, by the fountain, so I may present my case. Come alone, and I give you my word no harm will come to you.*

I turned the paper over, but could see no other message. I mused over this unconventional means of getting my attention. How had he even placed the message in my quarters? One of my servants must have brought it, and I felt slightly more at ease knowing that they had approved the letter.

Curiosity got the best of me, and I abandoned the rest of my lunch in favour of the mystery before me. I looked about the room to be sure I was unobserved, and I made my way down the curving stair to my walled garden. The stone pathways were close with the abundance of foliage and blooms, and friendly trees arched their limbs over the trails. I knew the way to the fountain, for it was a favourite spot of mine.

The fountain was a quarter-circular basin set in the corner of the garden wall, with a very old-looking relief carving of a fruit tree out of which water trickled and spilled down into the pool. Birds were fond of this place, and I loved the musical sound of the water mingled with their trills. But today, the birds were silent.

On the wide edge of the fountain's basin, the stranger sat. His hood was thrown back, now, and I saw the sheen of the noon light on his black hair. He watched me approach with a look I'd never seen before. I wasn't certain I liked it—I wasn't certain I didn't, either. My heart began to pound, though I didn't know why.

"Princess," the man said, rising and giving me a courtly bow. "Allow me to introduce myself. I am Leyukas, once the chief noble of this kingdom."

I halted in surprise. "I have never heard of you," I said frankly.

"I'm not surprised," he said with a small, almost bitter laugh. "Please, sit down, my Lady, and I will tell you my story, if you will allow it?"

I hesitated, but his charming smile put me at ease at once. I could see the man was unarmed, and I felt safe here in my garden. I smoothed my skirts out of the way and sat down on the edge of the fountain.

"As I said, I was once the chief noble, second in command only to Prince Kaehl himself. But there was a misunderstanding, and the Prince and I had a falling out." I frowned, taking new stock of this strange man and wondering what he was after. "I have no wish to malign the Prince, you understand," he said, holding out a hand of caution. "He is as blameless in this matter as I. It was merely a misunderstanding. But it grieves me to say he now holds me as his enemy."

Enemy. At the word, everything fell together in my mind. I rose hastily from the fountain and backed away against the wall.

"You?" I gasped. "You are Kaehl's enemy? He told me that you hated him, that you would stop at nothing to destroy everything he loves!" I was gathering my strength to flee at the slightest provocation, gathering my breath to scream.

Leyukas laughed heartily. "And here we find the misunderstanding." He held out his hands openly to show me that he meant no harm. The hammering of my pulse slowed, and I relaxed slightly, though I did not resume my seat.

"You have my ear for the moment," I said warily.

"Princess, you can see that I could have had you at my mercy here in this place, yet I have not and will not harm you. Take this example in good faith. I am not as Prince Kaehl thinks."

"Then what do you want?" I demanded.

"I seek reconciliation," he said simply. "I want to return to the palace and serve Prince Kaehl. But he will not see me, and he hunts me down relentlessly."

"You wish me to arrange this reconciliation? That is something I doubt I could do, even if I wanted to."

"I do not presume to ask that much. I only ask that you test the waters, to see if reconciliation is even possible."

"How would I do that?"

"Mention me to the Prince. See his reaction. You are a clever lady, Princess," he said with a smile. "You could ascertain very quickly if I have a chance, or not."

"Prince Kaehl is a reasonable man," I defended. "If there is no impediment, he will certainly hear your case."

"Perhaps," Leyukas said with a sceptical note. "I used to feel the same way, you know—I used to have such confidence in Prince Kaehl's character."

"And now?" I asked, with one arched eyebrow.

"Well, let's just say that I'd like things to go back to the way they were."

"I will ask him," I said with firm decision. After all, it was only a little, innocent question.

"Good," he said. "Then meet me in three days time to tell me his reaction."

"Where?"

"Do you know the pass of Rysha between the southern

mountains, the one that leads to the wood of Iffreyn?"

My blood froze, and I felt my heart flutter into my throat. Any place but that.

"I'm not permitted to go there," I whispered, breathless as I remembered the stricken look on Kaehl's face when he had found me in that clearing, in the shadow of the dark forest.

"Ah," he said with an expression that suggested he knew everything there was to know about this situation. "I beg your pardon if I am out of my place, but as Princess of the kingdom, are you not allowed to go wherever you wish?"

"Anywhere but there," I said simply. "Kaehl worries for my safety."

"But don't you see," he soothed, "I am the reason he worries. But you know now that you have nothing to fear from me. So it follows that if you are safe with me, then you are safe in the pass of Rysha."

"And yet I will not go there," I insisted.

"Alright," he conceded. "Would you meet me just below Iffreyn, then, so I am not required to go too far into Prince Kaehl's realm? I have taken a great risk to be here today."

"Fine," I allowed.

"In three days, then, Princess," he said with a bow. I looked down into the rippled water of the fountain, full of misgivings. Had I made the right choice? Surely Kaehl would approve of me taking initiative to heal his kingdom. When I looked up again, Leyukas was gone, with no trace.

—

"NO!!!"

My scream seemed to echo in the sparsely furnished bedroom.

84

"It's okay...You're safe, my Emma."

I curled in on myself within the safety of Cale's arms, trembling. *Leyukas. Lucas.* The name was synonymous with pure evil. Had I ever been so naïve as to believe otherwise? And yet, I knew I had. Only a month ago I had lived in ignorance, thinking of him as a benevolent father–figure—a saviour of sorts. How wrong I had been!

I wished I could tell my memory–self to run, to get the heck away from that hellish devil, no matter what his charms. His lies turned my stomach inside out, now that I knew the truth of them. But I was forced to keep on watching my memory play out the unravelling of my perfect past into my present mess.

—

Kaehl finally returned that evening. I greeted him with a grateful kiss, melting into his arms. After the events of the past few days, I was that much more relieved to see him again. Since he had been riding all day, he preferred to stay in the palace, and I suggested the fountain in my garden. I wasn't sure if it was because of Leyukas that I chose the place, or perhaps just because I had been reminded.

The birds were back to their singing as we entered the garden. I could see them splashing about in the basin, showering each other with liquid diamonds. It made my heart glad to see, and I nestled against Kaehl as we sat down together on the fountain's edge.

"Gavreyl tells me you were a wonder with the people today," he said, giving me a squeeze as I beamed. "They love you. You are truly a magnificent Princess." He laid a series of kisses in my hair and around the rim of my ear.

"I am only what you made me," I said, closing my eyes as I relished his attention. He rested against me, and I felt his weariness. He would never complain, never bring his cares to our times together, but I knew that his responsibilities weighed heavily on him. "Did you have a very difficult time today?" I asked, changing the subject.

He took a deep breath, and I knew he was deciding what to tell me.

"We heard rumours that...my Enemy...had been sighted in the East. We rode for half the day, only to find that he had sent one of his own servants as a decoy. It troubles me to wonder why."

I listened in silence, my mind working all the while. I knew exactly why Leyukas had sent the decoy—to draw Kaehl away and provide himself with an opportunity to speak with me alone. It was strange. When I spoke with Kaehl, I could only see this Enemy as a faceless Hate. But now that I had spoken to Leyukas, I had a face and a story to put to it, another side to the war and to the man I loved and thought I knew.

"What would you do, do you think, if this Enemy wanted peace with you?" I ventured, trying not to seem as if I held my breath.

I felt Kaehl go still. Had I upset him? Did he guess that I had spoken with that same Enemy just today, in this very spot? At last he answered me.

"I am a peaceable man, and I seek peace with everyone. But my Enemy has declared war on me in such a way that I doubt he would ever seek peace from me."

"But if he did?" I asked softly.

"If you understood this man as I do, my Immah, you

86

would know that it would be impossible. He is deceitful above all things, able to twist words so cunningly that many of the strongest of my knights have fallen to his banner. No, I do not think peace with him is possible."

I digested this quietly, for the first time in my existence wondering who I could trust. No matter what Kaehl said, I could not reconcile his image of Leyukas as a cold, lying, hating betrayer. Not now that I had met him. But I wouldn't betray Kaehl's trust in me. I would deliver the answer to Leyukas, as I had promised. Nothing more.

—

As the next three days progressed, I began to wonder how I was to deliver my message to Leyukas. Kaehl was not called away at all. Most of the time I simply forgot about my secretive errand, wrapped up in enjoying my future husband's company and helping him care for his kingdom. But at dawn on the third day, as I awakened, I heard the winding of horns. The warband was leaving.

"Was the Prince called away?" I asked my ladies as they came to dress me.

"Yes, Princess," Annayeh replied. "There was a rumour of trouble, and he is riding out with his men."

I sighed, remembering with dread the errand I must perform today. I worried less for Kaehl, knowing that in all probability Leyukas had drawn him away to free me to come. My beloved would meet with no harm. But I did feel uneasy about deceiving him. I was eager to have this deed over and done, and to move on with my life.

I planned my outing as if I were going for a picnic. It was a rest day, today, so there would be no petitions to deal with.

It would be perfectly normal for me to go for a ride, although I would usually have preferred to go with Kaehl. I was impatient to be gone, but I let none of it show as my ladies dressed me, and as I waited for my horse and provisions to be prepared.

At last I was mounted on my horse and turning southward once again, as I had vowed I never would. I took care not to overtax my horse this time, since I would need her to carry me home again before Kaehl returned. Thus it seemed to take forever before I reached the clearing before the forest of Iffreyn.

The sun sparkled on the sloping ground, dancing in the meadow flowers and the fluttering leaves of the friendly trees—such a stark contrast to the gloomy, unearthly stillness of the dark forest that loomed above. My horse snorted uneasily, and I tried to quiet her, dismounting and tying her to a branch. Then she reared up and pulled at her reins. In surprise, I looked behind me to see that I was no longer alone.

Leyukas stood in the clearing, as still and quiet as if he had simply appeared there rather than walking in. His appearance unnerved me, but I showed no signs. Then he put back his hood and smiled warmly, and the fear was replaced with a strangely foreign thrill.

"Princess, my thanks for your journey." He held out a hand to me, and I reluctantly gave him mine. To my surprise he kissed my fingers, and my pulse leaped. I looked at him in wide-eyed surprise.

"Does your Prince never do homage to your beauty?" he asked, startled.

"Of course he does," I answered. "But only he."

"Your pardon, my Lady," he smiled charmingly. "I will

behave better. Do you have an answer for me?"

"Yes, but I wish I could bring you a better one."

Leyukas's handsome face fell slightly. "I can't say I am surprised," he said, leading me by the hand across the meadow. "I expected this outcome. I assure you," he added, capturing my eyes in concern, "I will not attack your Prince—but you understand I must defend if he attacks me."

"Of course," I murmured, not liking the picture in my mind of Kaehl and Leyukas on opposite sides of the battle lines. I turned back to the north, where I could see the palace of Naeve gleaming white in the distant valley below. "I have done as you asked, and now I must return. The Prince wouldn't like me to be here."

"Do you mean here in this place, or here with me?" Leyukas asked in a smooth voice that made little fingers crawl up and down my back. He walked me around a bend, and I saw a blanket laid out with a feast. "Could you not stay and enjoy the fruits of your diplomatic mission? Call it a last moment of peace before the truce ends." He turned to me expectantly.

I hesitated. He was right–Kaehl wouldn't like me being here with *him*. But it was one meal, and then it would be over, for good. What harm could one meal do? And I was hungry after my morning's travel.

Leyukas settled me on the blanket, then sat down beside me to serve me. I had tasted delightful food before, and spent time in Kaehl's intoxicating company, but the meal I shared with Leyukas was something entirely new and different. He made me feel dizzy and afraid—in a good way, I decided. We spoke at length, and I found him drawing out of me experiences and feelings I never thought I'd share. He also had an uncanny way of knowing me. Before long, I had told him my entire story.

"So," he mused, "He made you for himself? To do his bidding and to kiss when it is convenient?"

"It's not like that," I said, blushing. "He treats me respectfully. He will marry me, he says, when the time is right."

"Ah, when the time is right. Now that is a saying I've heard many a time in Prince Kaehl's company. Although, I must admit, I'm surprised he hasn't taken you to wife—or at least to bed—yet. If you were my woman ..." he left the thought unspoken, though I could gather from the expression of relish on his face what he was thinking. Perhaps I should have been outraged, but his flattery produced a strange and powerful trembling in me. I couldn't think of anything to say in response.

"Forgive me, Princess," he said in his charming way. "I have spoken out of turn. I was simply wondering why he would make such misuse of you. Aside from the question of love and marriage, do you know he treated me much the same as you? I was his Vice–Regent in my day. He had me taking petitions and working as his clerk most of the time. I had some...suggestions about how we could run things differently, to maximize on the capabilities of the people and allow ourselves more latitude of time."

"Kaehl says that serving the people is our privilege," I said, frowning. "That we are connected to the kingdom."

"Does he?" Leyukas laughed. "Do you know he fed the same drivel to me? I realized before long he was just using that line to keep me working away for him. It's a sort of coerced slavery."

"I am hardly a slave," I said indignantly.

"Of course not, Princess," he said, his voice as smooth as a placid pool. His eyes were fixed on the crown upon my head. "Of course you aren't. You have a choice about everything you do. But then, it would be easier, don't you think, if he had just made you so no other choice occurred to you? Isn't it an awful burden to have to force yourself to choose what *he* wants?"

"I don't find it so onerous," I replied. "If Kaehl had made me with no choices, *then* I would be no better than a slave."

"Perhaps, but would you *know* you were a slave? It would never cross your mind to go into Iffreyn with me. But you, on the other hand, you do want to see what lies beyond that border. It is a choice, and a hard one, to stay within the limits Kaehl has set for you."

I looked over at the shadow of the dark trees, where it crossed the ground like a threshold.

"No," I insisted. "Kaehl loves me, and I love him. Love makes the choice easy."

"Love," he smiled. "Yes, love is powerful. And yet, Kaehl has shown you so little of what love has to offer." He gazed into my eyes, and I stared back like a fascinated bird, unable to look away. Before I knew it, Leyukas had leaned forward, closed the distance between us, and taken my lips with his.

I should have pulled away. I should have slapped him with all my force and fled. But I didn't. His hand slipped up my neck, under my hair, and held me close to him as he kissed me as Kaehl never had before. At the thought of Kaehl's name, Leyukas's spell slipped its hold, and I broke away, trembling.

"I love Kaehl," I whispered. "I love *him*." I repeated it, not so much to convince Leyukas as to convince myself.

"Go to him, then," Leyukas said, standing and pulling me

up with him. "Go and see if you were right, or I." He held out a hand to touch my face, letting his fingers trail down my neck and rest teasingly on my collarbone. "I could do so much more for you than he could, Princess," he said wistfully. "If you find that Kaehl is not enough for you, I am here, waiting, if you care to let your curiosity overcome your fear."

With wide eyes, I stepped away from him, then turned in search of my horse.

—

Fire lanced through my body. I threw up, aiming vaguely for the bowl. Then I turned into Cale's chest, sobbing and sobbing and sobbing.

5

I was safely home in the palace long before Kaehl arrived. We sat together at a late dinner, quiet and tense. Frustration emanated from him in palpable waves, and I knew the cause was Leyukas's decoy, but I was so wrapped up in my own confusion that I could not commiserate. How much sympathy could I give, after all, when I had begun to believe that Kaehl had brought this on himself? I could feel the divide between us, as though a wedge was driving its way in, forcing open a tiny crack of doubt.

I watched Kaehl as we ate, stealing secret glances as though by watching him unobserved I could gauge his heart of hearts. I wanted to believe that everything was as Kaehl had always told me. But Leyukas's words had the ring of truth, resonated with the tension that had already begun in me. The worst of it was that when Kaehl smiled at me, touched me, kissed me, his presence reminded me of Leyukas's.

I couldn't forget him. The thought of him waiting at the pass of Rysha, the thought of the kiss he'd left on me, made me restless. I couldn't fully enjoy Kaehl, and that wracked me with guilt. My questions whirled in my head, but I couldn't think how to ask them without offending Kaehl.

He was a good man, and I'd no intention of hurting him. I truly did want to be with him, forever. My heart ached at the thought of what he would feel if he ever knew what had transpired in the clearing today. He must never, ever know.

At the same time, my traitorous mind—and body—were still in that clearing, reliving the brief moments of Leyukas's touch, seeing his smouldering eyes on me. The memory was drawing me away from here, from the palace and Kaehl's arms. The guilt was pushing me away from the man I didn't feel I deserved. I was a woman torn in two.

"Something is wrong," Kaehl finally observed in his usual perceptive manner. He took a sip from his goblet of wine, effectively hiding the concern I knew was written across his face.

"I ..." I began, then looked away. "I'm flawed. You made me flawed."

He put down his goblet and was on his feet in an instant. He skirted the table and knelt on one knee next to me, taking my face in both his hands. His eyes flickered across my face, as though reading me like a book.

"What makes you think such a thing?" he asked.

"Nothing. Only, I ..." I couldn't bear to continue, couldn't meet his eyes.

"Immah, my Immah," he said. "Look at me. You are perfect in my eyes. You are everything I have ever wanted. You are everything to me."

"I want to believe you, Kaehl, I do." My voice broke. "But I—I want to disobey you."

He froze, and I could feel his eyes studying my face with increasing fervour.

"You met *him*, didn't you?" he asked. There was no accusation in his voice, no anger.

I nodded. "But he isn't what you say," I implored, only now glancing at his face. "He wants peace."

Kaehl's face darkened. "No, my darling, he doesn't. What he has done is declared open war on us, now, by seeking to turn you against me."

"He has done no such thing," I countered, though in the back of my mind I remembered Leyukas's kiss and my lips tingled with it.

"Hasn't he?" Kaehl asked softly, tracing my lips with his finger. Did he know, or only guess? "That is his way, you know. He has cornered me, for now I must either risk letting you run into danger with open arms, or risk painting myself as the villain by forcing you to obey. But I love you enough to risk everything, even losing your love.

"My Immah, you are my future wife. If you were anyone else, I wouldn't care so much. But you have promised to be mine, and I have a right to safeguard you. Please, if you love me, keep away from Leyukas."

I closed my eyes at the sound of the name. I wanted to promise, but I couldn't bring myself to say the words. I wrapped my arms around his neck and kissed him, letting the pent–up frustrations flood out of me through my lips. At last, Kaehl broke away and held me apart from him, his eyes bewildered.

"You've never kissed me like that before," he said.

"I want to be married, Kaehl," I said, more impatient than ever. I suddenly knew the solution—being Kaehl's wife would make me forget Leyukas and what he had done to my will.

"When the time is right," Kaehl said in a tone I used to find soothing.

In anger I threw off his arms and stood up, knocking the chair over. I stalked to the window.

"When, Kaehl?" I demanded. "When will the time finally be right? What is keeping you back?"

I rounded on him and found him staring, speechless. His eyes haunted me.

"I'm sorry," I said, my voice breaking. I held up my hands in surrender. "See? This is what I mean. I'm flawed."

"No," he said, crossing the room to me and gathering me into his arms. I let out my breath in a sob. "No, never." He whispered soothingly into my hair.

I gradually subsided, lulled by the irresistible force of his love.

—

Morning seemed to make everything new, bathing the world in honeyed sunshine. Kaehl met me for breakfast, and yesterday's troubles seemed to have vanished with the dawn mist. He was attentive and gentle, as always, and I wondered how I had ever doubted him.

But then, in the midst of our morning session in the throne room, Mikaehl came rushing through the masses to kneel at Kaehl's feet. I didn't have to hear their exchange to know what it meant. Kaehl glanced at me and lifted his eyes to the southern pass. His jaw set in grim determination. With a farewell kiss, he lifted up his sword from its place beside his throne, and strapped it around his waist as he strode purposefully out of the hall.

I ran to the window, with Gavreyl at one shoulder and Annayeh at the other, watching the warriors assemble and ride away to the south. I knew what this meant, and I couldn't decide whether I hated Leyukas for luring Kaehl away or feared for him in the face of my warrior prince's wrath. Only time would tell.

—

Time was something of which I had plenty, as it turned out. Hours turned into days, days into weeks. For nearly a month I watched and waited. No news came.

I tried to pour my heart into the people, as Kaehl would have wanted. But the hours of work seemed pointless without him. When I wasn't taking audience in the throne room, I was strolling listlessly in the garden or about the palace. I dared not ride out beyond the gates, for fear of the knowledge that I would surely go to the dark pass of Rysha.

I knew that my servants were concerned for me. My ladies plied me with diversions, and I could see Gavreyl watching me thoughtfully whenever he was near. No doubt he would have been reporting his observations to Kaehl, if he were here.

As time went on, I began to grow restless again. Leyukas's words began to creep in and supplant my sure knowledge of Kaehl's love. My work seemed arduous again, and Kaehl's slowness to marry me seemed proof that he did not love me.

At last, on a soft rainy day, I could stand it no more. I called for my horse and passed through the palace gates.

Gavreyl was waiting for me there.

"Please, Gavreyl," I implored his silent protest. "I must escape these four walls—I am going mad."

"Then allow me to go with you," he said patiently.

I shook my head. "I need to be alone. I promise you I'll be safe," I added.

"I can't advise you to ..."

All at once the weight of everyone's expectations grew too much. "As your Princess and Vice–Regent, I order you to let me pass."

Gavreyl stood aside, his face betraying surprise, and I spurred my mount. I had no care for holding back my speed this time. I had no thought of the return journey. I didn't even know what I planned to do.

I was drenched through by the time I arrived at the clearing, my wet hair and gown lashing me and snapping in the wind as I rode. I pulled on the rains and my horse wheeled around, whinnying loudly. The clearing seemed deserted, but I knew better. As I dismounted, I scanned the wood of Iffreyn, and I could see a dark figure beneath the trees.

"Leyukas!" I shouted. "What have you done to me?"

He stepped out into the dim light that was still bright in comparison to the forest. His hood slipped back onto his shoulders and he regarded me steadily. In the face of his gaze, my heart skipped crazily.

"I have done nothing—it is your heart that speaks to you. It will not let you rest until you acknowledge the truth."

"What truth?" I asked.

"You belong with me," he said simply. There was no moment of invitation, no conscious moment of choice. I began to move, to walk, to run, and then I was in his arms, finishing the kiss he had started nearly a month ago. This time I didn't stop.

"Come with me," he murmured, his lips still against mine.

I answered wordlessly, and he began to run, pulling me by the hand. The blood sang in my ears, coursing through me with dizzying speed. He led me across the border of the forest of Iffreyn, dragging me deeper and deeper into that blackness from which no light escaped. Even the stars in my crown seemed weak and their light watery, only illuminating a step or two ahead.

He led me to a little hollow that had a strange similarity to the place where Kaehl had made me. But it was so different—with twisted, gnarled trees rather than straight and tall, and pine needles instead of moss, and brambles in the place of flowers, and darkness instead of dancing sunshine—that the place did not resurrect any memories of Kaehl. Not now, with Leyukas beside me.

He took me down to the ground, kissing me and gripping me close, and I was lost.

—

There were hands on me. Someone's breath in my ear. I flailed against the grasping fingers, writhed away from the gentle words.

"Emma, it's okay. It's me, Cale!"

"No! Don't touch me! Leyukas, stop it! I didn't mean it!"

The touches stopped, but my skin still burned with them.

—

It didn't take very long for me to realize I had made the gravest mistake. Perhaps it was early on, when Leyukas's tenderness and passion transformed into roughness and degradation. Perhaps it was after, as I lay curled on the prickly carpet of pine needles, cradling my memories of Kaehl's love and my imaginings of his certain broken heart. But the moment I knew for sure I had made a mistake was when Leyukas rose, dusted off the clinging detritus from his smooth pale skin, and looked down on me with a steady, mocking gaze of exultation. Then, he left me.

Trembling, and strung much too tight even to weep, I gathered my torn and dirty white gown and put it on. My fumbling fingers missed the catches, without the usual help from my ladies, so I soon gave up and covered the gaping dress with my cloak. I staggered to my feet and wandered in the rough direction I remembered Leyukas bringing me. Curse the man! Everything Kaehl had said about him was right. But now it was too late. He had used me.

No, maybe not too late. I had made a mistake—but I had learned. I saw the faint glow of light ahead, the pearl grey light of the rainy clearing. I would ride home, as fast as I could. I would go to my room, wash away all trace of this day's disgrace, and pretend it had never happened.

I managed to mount my horse despite my shaking legs, and coax it to a swift speed toward the palace. I couldn't wait to put as much distance as possible between me and that dark, horrifying wood. But the closer I came to home, the more vivid came the memories of what had transpired in that hollow, that twisted mockery of the place where Kaehl had made me.

I made it into the palace with my hood up over my hair, so no one could see the terror on my face. If my ladies had questions when I asked them to leave me alone, they did not say. I was grateful. I could not draw a bath without attracting notice, so I went out into the garden and scrubbed what my clothes didn't cover with the cold water in the fountain. I wished the tears would stop, so I could wash those away, too.

I changed into a fresh white gown. It seemed strange to see something so white against my skin, as though merely by touching it I might make it, too, dirty. My torn and filthy dress was more of a problem. I couldn't dispose of it without anyone seeing, so I took it into the garden and buried it behind a large, thick rose briar.

Then I took up my vigil, watching by the window hoping for Kaehl to come home, but hoping I would never have to face him and tell him what I had done.

—

"She won't come out," someone said on the other side of the door. "She hasn't been anywhere but her chambers for the past three days. She won't have anyone in, either."

"She'll have me," someone else said, his voice grim. Kaehl! I turned to the door in horrified longing. I had been so deep in my dark thoughts that I hadn't heard the clamour of his arrival. I rose quickly from my chair and began to pace the room. The door began to open.

"No, no!" I cried, hurrying away to my bedchamber and closing the door. "I'm ill! I can't see you." I cringed behind the door, my pulse racing and my lips trembling with fresh tears to come.

"Immah," came an infinitely tender voice from the other side of the heavy wood. I pressed my cheek against the sound. "Let me in. I know."

I froze, unable, or unwilling, to ask what it was that he knew.

"I know *everything*." His voice, though still soft, conveyed all the betrayal and anguish that I had expected, and more. I couldn't open the door, but I moved away to sit on the bed with my head turned toward the wall and my knuckles pressed against my mouth.

I could feel him in the room with me—his presence seemed to fill up the space like water filled a vessel. I noticed he didn't touch me. He didn't speak for a long while, and finally I gathered my courage to look up at him. It was a mistake. I had a brief impression of his eyes, shadowed and haunted by my cruelty, before my own eyes filmed over with tears.

"I might ask you why," he said softly, and now I could tell that his voice was hoarse, "But it wouldn't matter."

The weeping started then, and I was carried away by grief. The worst of it was the complete sense of isolation as he stood aloof and watched me cry. He couldn't touch me. I knew that now. It wouldn't be seemly for him to touch me, now that I was sullied.

"I was wrong, Kaehl," I sobbed. "I was wrong, and I'm sorry. I'm sorry." The last words barely came out of my mouth as my throat constricted. "Can't you forgive me?"

"Immah," he said, his breath coming out in a rush. "Oh, my Immah!" he sat down beside me and his arms were around me in an instant. I curled gratefully into the hollow of his shoulder, my tears releasing in a torrent. "Oh, but I wish it were that easy."

Something in his voice made me stop, to pull away and look at his face. But his eyes had gone far away and his face like stone. Before I could ask him anything, I heard a sound that chilled me. I had never heard it before, but I knew what it was—the deep drone of the monstrous alarm horn. Someone was invading.

I jumped to my feet and ran to the window. Kaehl stood more slowly, heading for the door. He had expected this. I felt all colour drain from my face as I chased after him.

I was full of questions as I followed him through the corridors. He seemed to gather inertia as he walked, so that he appeared larger, more substantial. I thought he might have smashed right through a solid oak door without slowing. It frightened me to think of that wrath turned against me.

He did not slow until he reached the ramparts. As I followed him closely, his bulk shielded everything from my view. But when he stopped, I fell into place beside him, and I gasped.

Every enemy Kaehl had ever had must have assembled at the gates. At his appearance they began to call their taunts, brandishing their weapons. They were every bit as grotesque and horrifying as Kaehl's army was noble and elegant. And at their head, Leyukas stood.

"Come down, Kaehl!" he shouted in a voice twisted with hate. "Come down and give me what is mine by right!"

At first, I didn't understand what Leyukas meant. But then, when Kaehl took my hand in bleak silence, it dawned on me.

"Me?" I shrieked, snatching my hand back. "He wants me?! No! You can't give me to him! Please, Kaehl! Have mercy!"

I fled to a corner of the battlement, searching in vain for some hold in the smooth white stone to cling to. But there was no stopping my beloved. He lifted me up as though I weighed nothing and walked slowly to the stair.

"Please don't do this, Kaehl!" I wept as I struggled. "Please!"

"I must," Kaehl said, and I could hear the emotion in his voice, barely under control. "Please understand. You have chosen this."

I went still, then, burying my face into his shoulder. "No," I whispered. This was the last time he would hold me. The thought was unbearable. I inhaled deeply of his scent, mingled with my tears. "Please. I love you."

He set me on my feet, just inside the gate. His fingertips

brushed my face, and I closed my eyes.

"I love you, too," he said. "You cannot fathom how much I love you. This is how it must be." My eyes stung with tears, and my breath caught in panic. "But don't despair, my Immah," he went on, and hope rose fleetingly inside me. "I will come for you. I will do whatever it takes to win you back," he leaned close to my ear, his lips brushing my hair, "Even if it takes my life."

My fingers clutched at his robes as he walked me out to meet Leyukas. I wondered how I ever could have found this terrible man attractive. Now, I cowered at the sight of him. But he was my master now.

"Go, now, Immah," Kaehl said softly. "But remember my promise."

I nodded. He kissed me once more—far too fleetingly— and gently disengaged my fingers from his clothes. I could see he didn't want to part from me any more than I did from him. I gathered all the dignity I could muster and turned to walk toward my awful overlord. I looked over my shoulder at Kaehl, standing alone. Though he looked as majestic as ever, to me he seemed forlorn.

Then I was before Leyukas, and I felt his hands close around my arms in triumph. He said no word—he had no need. I was his now, and everyone knew it.

His men let out a mighty, ear-shattering victory roar as Leyukas lifted me up onto his horse like so much baggage. Then I was carried away to the dark pass in the south, watching Kaehl's palace diminish in the distance through tear-flooded eyes.

The ride was a nightmare of noise and jostling and Leyukas's lascivious touches. I shuddered, remembering that I had invited this. And then there was the voice, soft as velvet and harsh as nails on slate crooning in my ear.

"You didn't think you could give yourself to me and take it all back, did you? You're mine now—you and everything that comes with you. Kaehl will pay for what he did to me. And you will bear that price. Come, my beautiful Immah, and let's see if we can't enjoy sweet revenge for eternity."

His voice made me sick. Too soon, he was swinging me down from the saddle by my arm, twirling me around roughly against his body in the close soundlessness of Iffreyn. I whimpered. He held my head in his hands, and I was both afraid and hopeful that he might crush me or break my neck. But the eternity of torture was only beginning. He lifted my crown from my head, pulling my hair painfully in the process.

As I watched in horror, my delicate gold circlet with its shining stars morphed into a twisted iron crown with cold, lightless diamonds. His eyes alight with exultation, Leyukas put the crown on his head. Nothing could have prepared me for what happened next.

The ground began to shake violently. I screamed and fell to my knees, not willing to reach out to Leyukas for support. Trees were uprooted. The sky grew dark, and a high wind stirred the clouds like boiling water. The tops of the trees bent down and snapped. Then there was a mighty cracking sound as though the earth was rending in two.

When the quaking finally ceased, I staggered to my feet. Leyukas looked down on me with a cruel smile on his face, and I was overwhelmed with the desire to flee. I turned from him and ran back toward my valley, toward Kaehl. I heard him laughing behind me as I fought through the clutching brambles, and I expected that my escape was futile.

He did not pursue me, though, and I had a fleeting hope that I might succeed. I could see light ahead. The clearing came into view, and I burst out into the open, breathing deeply of the air. But when I looked about me, I understood the laughter, and the lack of pursuit. There was no where to run, anymore. The valley of Parras, the palace of Naeve, the mountains, the river, Kaehl—it was all gone.

In its place was a barren wasteland, a crude mockery of Parras. In the centre of the dusty plain stood a ziggurat, jagged and squat and grey. From the peak of the stepped pyramid flew a banner, black as a starless night, with Leyukas' crimson sign proud and cruel upon it.

—

I sat in the clearing for a long while alone, watching the transformed landscape bleakly and listening to the wild jubilation of Leyukas's dark warhost as they poured down the mountainside toward the ziggurat. I hugged my knees to me, stroking the soft silken shreds of my once–white gown. I believed that Kaehl meant his promise to save me, but I didn't know how long that might take, or if it was even possible, now that the world was broken and Parras was gone. I was beyond weeping, beyond fleeing, beyond responding to any of this.

Even when Leyukas came up behind me I didn't move. I felt his hand slide down my tangled hair and over my shoulder, but I restrained the urge to throw off his hand. I would become like stone, and feel none of this. I would be as one dead, only to come alive again when Kaehl returned for me.

A cup appeared before my face, looming close to my

lips, and only then did I flinch away. But Leyukas's iron hand gripped the back of my neck and forced the rim of the cup to my lips. He poured it over my clenched lips, into my nostrils, until I had to open my mouth and drink, or be drowned.

Then he let me go with a rough shove of satisfaction, and I collapsed sideways with a gasp. I lay there alone for an age, with the drugged drink drying on my chin and staining my white dress crimson. I stared up at the alien grey sky, with the stunted, twisted trees waving above me. I shivered, I wept, I curled into a ball until my muscles seized.

I could feel the drug taking hold of me, one little insidious tendril at a time. It relaxed my muscles. It stopped the flow of my tears. It warmed my cold body. And most unforgivable of all, it crept into my mind and removed my memories, one by one. I railed against its work for a time, but before long I was powerless. Not only was Kaehl physically gone, now it would be as if he had never even existed.

I felt the deep sadness of despair wash over me as I lay in the empty clearing, and I didn't even know why.

—

Ambrosia. I could taste that first dose on my lips, and my throat burned for it. My veins screamed at me. *Ambrosia. Ambrosia. Ambrosia!* With every beat of my heart it grew louder, more insistent.

"Please! Cale! Sloane! Lucas! Give it to me!!" I shrieked. I threw my arms out in violent protest, connecting with something solid. Arms wrapped around me and I struggled harder, screaming at the tenderly annoying voice in my ear.

My vision blurred and turned black, as my whole body stiffened.

—

The flow of memories grew jumbled then, now vivid, now faint, all disjointed. I had an impression of years, of centuries, millennia, even. I stood at Leyukas's side in China, Sumer and Mesopotamia, I crouched in his shadow in ancient Palestine and Egypt, in India and the Mayan Empire. I was a temple prostitute in Persia, Babylon, Greece and Rome. I slaved for him in a Viking hall, in a Castle scullery. I sailed with him as he plundered the rich and poor over every sea imaginable. I inhabited his dark underworld in burgeoning cities of London, Paris, and New York. I was a pawn in the beds of princes and kings. I watched him amass his fortunes again and again, ever controlling principalities and powers from the sidelines, and always the world belonged to him.

Through it all, I remained in my Ambrosia–driven stupor. At times I had a sense of my immortality, though I dismissed the idea as a fantasy. I had an impression that there was something more to this life, something I waited for. But I couldn't remember what it was that fuelled my longing. I never imagined in all of my dreams that a shining prince waited for the right time to return to me from his inaccessible Otherworld.

6

I came to myself gradually, understanding that the words I mumbled belonged to a different place and time than the one in which I existed. There were tears, both dried and fresh, on my face. My hair was knotted and sweaty. My body ached and throbbed. My mouth tasted putrid. I was as weak and flaccid as a sick newborn.

Then I was conscious of arms, strong and solid, around me, and I knew that was the only real thing in my world. I rolled into them, nuzzling into a warm, muscular chest. I could feel his breath in my hair, catching now and then with emotion. Cale.

I looked up into his eyes, focusing for the first time on my beloved now that I knew him. There was no crown, no robes, no heraldry, but he bore the unmistakeable stamp of a prince. Besides that, the differences were few but astounding. His hair was shorter, he was clean-shaven, his clothes modern, but that was minor. It was the intangible things that stood out— the deep hollows under his grey–green eyes, the grief lines on his face, the leanness of his frame. I knew I had caused these, and I wept afresh.

"Oh Kaehl! Cale!" I cried, hiding my face from him. "I'm sorry. I'm so sorry!"

"Shh," he hushed me, brushing back my sweaty hair. "It's alright now. I'm here. It'll be okay."

"You promised," I said in wonder. "You promised, and I forgot. You came."

"Of course I came," he said, his voice rough with emotion. He kissed me deeply.

I pulled away.

"What's wrong?" he asked.

"Ugh, my breath must be awful!"

"I don't care!" He laughed and kissed me again, wrapping me tightly in his arms. Then he simply held me against him. "I'm so glad to have you with me again. So glad you *know* me again!"

"It's like I've been to death and back," I mused.

"You very nearly did. Did you know you had a seizure?"

"But I'd do it gladly a hundred times for you."

"Would you?" he asked.

"Yes!" I retorted, not sure I liked his sad tone. "I've learned my lesson."

He traced my jaw gently with his fingertips. We lay like that for a long while, forgetting the world that waited, the friends in the other room, the dark lord who undoubtedly was searching for me. But although we had forever, the needs of the body would not be ignored. My stomach growled loudly, effectively ending our bliss for now.

"I'll get you something to eat," Cale said, jumping up from the bed. "You wait here." Then he disappeared.

I may have been weak and stiff from who knew how long in that bed, but I wasn't about to lie there any longer. I struggled out of the tangled sheets, grimacing at the occasional bit of mess that had missed the bowl. Then I hobbled slowly across the room and down the hall, holding onto the furniture.

When the men in the living room saw me, they jumped up off the couch. Mike was already picking me up off my feet when Cale poked his head disapprovingly out of the kitchen. Gabe produced a pillow, and the two of them got me settled on the couch. From what I could see, it was the middle of the night. The TV showed some infomercial that no one was watching, and it was dark outside. Which night it was, though, I had no idea.

The men asked no questions, but they seemed both pleased and concerned to see me. I decided to volunteer.

"Mikaehl, Gavreyl," I said, nodding to each one, "My thanks for helping Cale save me. I owe you both my life."

"The credit belongs to Cale," Mike said gruffly, and Gabe nodded his agreement.

"We are only happy to have our Princess returned to us," Gabe said.

As Cale entered with a tray of food, the two men bowed out, headed for the bedrooms. I imagined the only person more tired than they were was Cale.

"They are both very fond of you, you know," Cale said as he sat down beside me. "Especially Gabe. They wouldn't hear of my coming to save you without their company."

"I'm glad. I wouldn't want you to be alone."

"Hmm," Cale said, distracting me with a spoonful of soup, though I didn't miss the shadow that flitted across his eyes.

I ate in silence for a while, grateful to enjoy food truly for the first time in aeons, but careful not to upset my very empty stomach. Cale didn't seem to mind. Our silence was comfortable, and I hadn't experienced that in so long. Until now, silence had always reminded me of the questions that I couldn't

111

remember, let alone answer.

"I have so many questions," I voiced aloud, then yawned widely.

"That can wait till tomorrow," Cale replied, helping me to lay flat. "After you sleep."

I couldn't complain, and let myself drift into a sleep untainted by Ambrosia, for the first time filled with real dreams.

—

It was late morning, or maybe afternoon when I awakened again, back in the bed. The sheets had been changed, and there seemed to be no trace of the marks of my epic struggle. Someone, probably Cale, had carried me from the couch and tucked me in. I sat up, catching a glimpse of myself in the mirror with a moue of distaste.

My hair was greasy and sticking out every which way. My clothes were rumpled and stained. I had no makeup on, and I was pale and wan with dark smudges under my eyes. But I knew that Cale loved me, even like this. My grimace turned into a bright smile.

I rolled out of bed and rose on unsteady feet. Still smiling, I rummaged in the drawer and pulled out a pair of jeans and a white shirt. With the clothes slung over my arm, I tottered off to the bathroom to wash. It felt so good to clean away the last of the Ambrosia's effects. Its hold was broken, and now it was nothing but a memory, as of a half–forgotten bad dream.

Cale must have heard me in the shower, because he was ready when I came out, a big breakfast ready on a tray. The three men stood when I came in.

"Good morning, Princess," they all said in turn. The world seemed brighter, more beautiful, like I was looking through the proverbial rose-coloured glasses. I had been asleep for so long in that awful nightmare of Lucas's creation, and now I was finally awake. Cale had awakened me.

I greeted them all, stopping to embrace and kiss Cale before I sat down. There was something different—something I had seen but not realized ever since the effects of the Ambrosia had worn off. The way I saw was different. I knew it wasn't just the glow of happiness. I could see almost like a faint shadow, if I could call it that, for it seemed lighter rather than darker, that overlaid each of the men in the room. I noticed it more when I relaxed my eyes or looked away than if I stared and concentrated, much like faint stars are brighter in peripheral vision.

I was about to write it off as some strange side-effect of my recent trauma, but when I sat down at the table, I caught sight of a brilliant flash of light. It came from Cale's forehead, where his star-set crown should have been. I gasped.

"What is that?" I asked. "What am I seeing?"

Cale smiled and covered my hand with his where it gripped the edge of the table.

"It's Otherworld," he said.

The word made the little hairs stand up on my arms and the back of my neck. I actually thought I heard the sound of a breeze rustling in leaves, and smelled a revenant scent of an orchard in bloom.

"What do you mean?" I demanded, thoroughly amazed and a little freaked out by this time.

"Eat," Cale said, pointing at my laden plate. "And then I'll tell you."

Obediently, I picked up my fork and filled my mouth, looking up at him with large, curious eyes as I chewed.

"When...my Enemy...took you," and even now the words were hard for him to say. I looked down in shame. "The world was torn. I couldn't let him ruin my whole kingdom, so I carved a piece of it away and made it so no one could pass from this world to Otherworld. But I have to tell you, it was like cutting off my own limb, especially since you were on the other side."

I looked at him in dismay. I couldn't find words for the heartache I felt at what I had done. But he cupped my chin in his hand and kissed me.

"I know what you're thinking," he said. "But don't worry. I love you. I'll make a way for you." A shadow darkened his eyes for a moment, and I tilted my head quizzically. But then I caught a glimpse of that strange other–Cale within his face.

"There it is again!" I said, distracted. "How is it I can see Otherworld, when it's broken away from this world?"

"You are different from Lucas and his minions," Cale said. "You belong there, although he took great pains to make sure you never knew it, thanks to that drug. But now that it's gone, you are beginning to see the world you were meant to belong to. You are a true Otherworlder. You were made for it, and it for you. You will go back there someday.

"But you see, this world can't be glued together with Otherworld like if I had broken off a corner of this table. It has to be woven, like a fabric. With me here, the threads are beginning to interlace, and you are beginning to see it. It's like looking at something through water."

I watched in wonder as the emblem of his kingdom appeared on his chest and faded again. I could see—it was as he had told me, so long ago. Otherworld was like that knotwork, all interconnected. Yet, as I compared this world with the kingdom I remembered, I couldn't reconcile the two.

"Okay, so you want to make this world a part of Otherworld again? But isn't this world a lost cause? It seems too broken to fix!"

"It's never a lost cause—don't say that." He held my hands tightly in his vehemence. "You weren't a lost cause. No, this world is a big mess—Lucas made certain of that the moment he took this land, and you, from me. But I intend to win it back, one inch at a time."

"How do we do that?" I asked, somewhat daunted. "How do we weave it all back together?"

"You'll see," he said with a slight grim cast to his mouth that did nothing to banish my apprehension.

—

The next day, Cale took me out. It was my first time out of the apartment since he had rescued me, which had been, as it turned out, five days ago. I felt silly, blinking at the bright daylight as we rolled out of the parking garage. Mike drove us out of the city, and I felt more and more at ease as I saw the tall buildings recede in the distance.

The sensation was strange. On the one hand, until recently, the city had been the only home I could remember. If someone had tried to take me away from here before I had regained my memories, I would have kicked and screamed. But on the other hand, now that I had a memory of Otherworld, and sharing nature with Cale aeons ago, I was eager for the open spaces and the smell of fresh air again.

We flew past the suburbs, and out into the country, and as the hours passed in happy companionship, we turned off the highway onto a dirt road that led beyond the big commercial farms to the little corners of land that time had forgotten. There were little old cottages nestled here and there amid woods and overgrown gardens, and rolling, stony hills that yielded only enough for subsistence. Further on, we turned down a narrow lane that had once been gated.

As we turned a bend in the lane, I could see what had once been a grand estate, all gables and nooks and crannies, overhung with ivy and climbing roses. The house was set on a hill, with very old trees and green lawns all around. A flock of sheep ran from the relative noise of our car, cascading down the smooth hillside like cotton balls rolling across green velvet.

I pressed my face to the glass, taking it in with wonder.

"What is this place?" I asked.

"It's the home of a friend," was all Cale would say. "He owes me a favour."

As we pulled up to the door, a spry old man hobbled down the stairs to meet us. He had the kind of bright eyes and inquisitive wrinkled face that brought out a spontaneous smile in me. I had never met anyone quite like him before.

"Emma, this is Simon," Cale introduced. "Simon, I believe you know Emma."

The old man clapped his frail fingers around my hand, his expression bursting with joy. "So I do! So I do! But you won't know *me*, my dear. I have been waiting for this day for a very, very long time!"

I looked quizzically at Cale, but he just smiled proudly and shrugged. He put his large, warm hand on the small of my back in a pleasantly proprietary way.

"Welcome to Avenham! Come in, come in," Simon said,

turning and tottering back up the stairs he had just descended. "Annie has some soup on, and I'll tell her to start the tea."

He led us into the house, chattering all the way through the enormous front hall and disappearing through a small side passageway. At Cale's urging, I followed, catching glimpses here and there of grand rooms, some standing empty, some filled with anonymous cloth–covered shapes of furniture. Simon puttered into a large, bright kitchen, redone sometime in the 1950s with mint green painted, now peeling, cabinets and black and white linoleum floor. There was a long, scarred oak table against one wall, with mismatched painted chairs around it.

A woman just as old and frail as Simon stood at the counter, clad in a dress and red apron. She turned as Simon entered and her face lit up with surprised joy.

"Oh! You're here already," she cried. "Simon, why didn't you call me?"

"I would, m'dear," he said affectionately, "But you're stone deaf and you wouldn't have heard me even if I'd the breath to shout. So I'm telling you now. They're here." He swept his arm out to indicate the four of us, a cheeky smile on his winter–apple face.

The woman who must be Annie favoured him with a frown, but it soon vanished, replaced by a smile for us. She came across the room with surprising grace and speed for her age, her arms outstretched to embrace Cale. Then she pulled Mike and Gabe into her arms, too. With a motherly pat on each of their cheeks, she then turned to me.

"I've waited for this day for a very long time," she said softly, her eyes gone misted with tears. She was a tiny thing, and she had to look up to see me, but she raised her papery hands to frame my face. I held very still, not sure how to behave. "And I know Cale has too."

At the mention of Cale, my eyes darted to his face and back to Annie. It hadn't occurred to me how many others knew about my betrayal, and how it might have affected them. My cheeks burned with shame.

Cale put an arm around me protectively as Annie gently removed her hands.

"Never mind about that," he whispered for only me to hear. "I've got it covered."

Gratitude flooded me as I followed him to the table. Annie was bustling around, putting out bowls filled with soup and a piping hot chicken pie in the middle of the table. We ate in real companionship, and I listened to the friends sharing stories and happy memories. I had never felt so at ease before, so at home—at least, not since Otherworld. I still felt a niggling unease, as though it was all too good to be true, but I put it aside, determined to enjoy this fairy tale.

After lunch, Simon took us for a walk while Annie washed up. I offered to help, but she clucked her tongue at me and waved me away. For a while, Simon talked about the estate, sharing fascinating bits of its history, but soon his talk turned to matters I didn't understand that seemed to absorb Cale, Mike, and Gabe. I only caught snippets of what they were saying as I lagged behind, soaking in the beauty of the grounds.

"What comes next?" Simon asked Cale at one point.

"First, I train her," he answered, and my ears perked up with interest.

"A sound idea. But do you have the time?"

"Time enough," Cale said with a heavy sigh. "I can't simply leave her defenceless."

Leave her? My heart began to pound in a panic. No! Cale couldn't leave me, not now.

"And...*him*?" Simon asked, his voice dropping into a hissing whisper.

"It's not like you think. I can't explain right now." Cale's voice was unsettlingly troubled. Simon looked thoughtful but didn't say anything. I didn't like that. Cale was my rock, my unshakeable tower in the middle of a world that was falling apart. He couldn't be crumbling, too. I needed him to be strong.

The conversation turned to other things, but I didn't forget the worrisome implications of what I'd heard. Could I ask Cale about it later? I wasn't sure I wanted to hear the answer.

As it turned out, there wasn't a chance. When we returned to the house, Annie showed me to my room, a fantastic suite that was more of an apartment of its own. There was a large sitting room with a fully semi–circular bow window that overlooked the front of the house, a bedroom through panelled double doors, and a bathroom with a large claw–foot tub in the middle.

"Take your time," Annie said with a wink. "Enjoy the place. Cale seemed to think you'd be wanting some time on your own to rest."

It was true. While I did long for Cale's company every minute, I had been through a lot in a short time, with no time to digest it all. I turned on the water in the tub, then wandered the rooms for a few minutes while it filled. The suite must have been more sparsely decorated than it had once been, as generations found the upkeep of the antiques harder and harder, but it didn't look empty. There were plenty of curiosities left—most of which I began to recognize as familiar now that I had my centuries–long memory back. I found many an item just like ones I had owned myself, once upon a time, when they had been new.

The place was fantastic, really in great shape for the age it must be. The wood floors were polished like glass, punctuated with carefully preserved antique rugs. The ceilings were painted with scrollwork in between carved oak rafters. The furnishings were a mishmashed timeline of history from the Renaissance to the Regency. It was a place that rivalled even the finest apartments Lucas had put me in.

The thought of that name brought an immediate reaction in me. All other processes seemed to stop at once, my breathing, my heartbeat, whatever train of thought that might otherwise have formed. I hadn't thought of him, not really, since I'd wakened free in Cale's arms. He had been nothing more than a shadow, a distant nightmare to haunt my waking hours. Once I had broken free of the Ambrosia, my memory of him was of Leyukas, that monstrous deceiver long ago. But I had conveniently put out of my mind the man who lived now, in the city we'd just left. The man who was looking for me.

Millennia of memories flooded my mind at once—memories of beatings and of degradations, of lies and drugged sleep. I ran for the bathroom and heaved into the toilet as if I could expel that horrible mess from my memory the way my lunch left my body. Wiping my mouth grimly, I turned off the taps. I knew the bath wouldn't help. I wasn't sure anything would, though, so I got into the hot water anyway.

No, there was one thing that could help, but it was out of reach. And I certainly didn't want Ambrosia again, not anymore. I wished I could convince my jangling nerves of that same thing.

—

Cale knew at once that something was wrong when I finally wandered downstairs. I should have known he would. Without a word, just a glance at my face, he threw his arms around me and walked me out of the kitchen into a little wood-panelled nook in the hall. I could feel everyone's eyes watching me as we left, their ears straining to hear what we might say, no doubt wondering what was wrong. Or perhaps they knew already. That thought filled me with renewed shame.

Cale didn't ask. He just held me and waited, stroking my hair while I shook. I couldn't even cry. But gradually his patient love stilled me, calmed me. I could almost feel it like a tangible thing, like a cloak coming to rest over my shoulders. I felt like his love could repel anything that might attack me. It made me invincible.

I raised my eyes to him, only now glistening with tears, filled with wonder at his power over me. And it wasn't the kind of power that Lucas—and even now I couldn't think the name without shuddering—had exerted over me. He had once bullied and manipulated, cajoled and downright beaten his will into me. But Cale's power was effortless and gentle—a power he could have taken for himself, but wouldn't wield unless I gave it to him. Wrapped securely in his arms, under the soothing influence of his tenderness, I felt freer than I ever had before. Not even in the idyllic days of Otherworld had I known this feeling. Now I truly knew freedom, because I had experienced the bonds of captivity.

"Thank you," I murmured, kissing Cale gratefully.

"What happened?" he asked, rubbing the tension out of my shoulder.

"I don't really know. One minute I was so happy, and the next I felt so bleak ..."

"It was *him*?" Cale asked.

I nodded. "I remembered everything he'd done to me, and ..." I choked a little on the words. "I felt ashamed, and afraid, and for a minute I wanted the Ambrosia to wipe it all away again. That scared me more than anything. Because I don't want to lose you, Cale, I don't!" I buried my face into his shoulder, breathing deeply.

"You won't, my love, my Emma, not now." He kissed my hair, gathering me close.

"I'm still afraid, Cale," I whispered, seeking his eyes. "What will we do?"

"About *him*?" Cale asked, though we both knew what I meant. "Nothing yet. You have things to learn first."

"Will we be okay, though?"

"Of course," he smiled, tracing my hairline as he gazed down at me. "He can't touch us here. I've made it safe."

I didn't know how he could possibly know that for sure. But it was hard not to trust in his strength, and I was swept up in his optimism. Freedom, at last!

"Now, my Emma," he said, dropping his arms and catching up my hand with a light kiss. "You need something to eat, and then tomorrow we begin to train you."

"Train me?" I blinked. "*Me*? To fight?"

"Yes, *you*," he said with a chuckle. "To fight."

—

"A sword?" I asked dubiously, eyeing the gleaming—and archaic—weapon that rested in Cale's hands.

"A sword," he confirmed, holding it out to me with a raise of his eyebrows. I knew he meant me to take it, but I shrank back reluctantly. It was double–edged, about 3 inches wide, and the length of my arm. Granted, it was pretty, with interlaced designs engraved down the blade and around the shining silver and white hilt. It looked razor sharp.

We were in a quiet clearing far from the manor house, far from anything, in fact. It was not long after dawn, and mist crept between the boles of ancient trees, making me feel as if we really could have been back in our rightful home.

"But I didn't have to fight before, in Otherworld," I protested, looking for any excuse to avoid making a fool of myself.

"Everything is different now," Cale said gently. "Before, there wasn't a need."

That stung, since the only reason there was a need now was because of my treachery. Part chastened, part challenged, I reached out decisively and took the grip. I met Cale's eyes with the slightest smile as I hefted the sword in my hand.

It was surprisingly light for such a sturdy blade. I tried out a few clumsy, slow–motion practice swings in spite of my self–consciousness, and Cale had the grace not to laugh at me.

"I'm not in very good shape, you know," I said with a laugh. I almost continued with an excuse: *Lucas likes to keep his girls scrawny.* But I bit my tongue and instantly sobered. I had to remember what I was fighting for.

Cale pulled out his own sword, giving a grave nod at the new resolve he saw emblazoned on my face. He raised the tip of his blade to a defensive position and crouched a little. I imitated him, and when I felt like laughing at myself, I kept Lucas's face before me as a galvanizing force.

"We'll go easy at first," Cale said. "Build you up a bit. Start by imitating me, like a dance. We'll begin slowly, add it bit by bit, then speed it up. Okay?"

I nodded, not taking my eyes from his.

Cale did start easy. First he lifted his blade up over his right shoulder, extending it diagonally downward until his elbows were straight. I copied. He stepped forward, thrusting the sword–point ahead. I copied. He did the same thing from left to right. I copied. I began to feel not only like I could do this, but that I might even get bored by it. Was he insulting my intelligence?

But after repeating simple, slow movements like this for a half–hour, I began to see the point. The sword that had seemed so light at the beginning now seemed ten times heavier. My muscles, which had found the movements easy and fluid, now strained and burned. And my memory began to play back the pattern for me, until I could do each movement in sync with Cale, side by side.

Then, when my body could take no more of this slow motion, Cale told me to speed it up. My muscles, though tired, responded with almost joyous vigour. My arms and legs knew their part instinctively, and I found I was free to concentrate on other things—the flash of sun on our swords, the miniscule rises and dips in the land under my feet, the perfectly clear focus in Cale's grey–green eyes.

We broke for lunch, and Cale walked me to a nearby brook. He bent to splash water on his face, while I merely collapsed on a flat moss–covered rock. Turning to look at me, he laughed.

"You're doing well, you know," he said with a smile, carefully bringing a double–handful of water to me to drink. After I sipped, he took his cool wet hands and smoothed my hair back from my face. I closed my eyes and sighed.

"Something tells me I'm not even close."

"You let me worry about that," he said, lying down on his back beside me. He held out his arm for me to cuddle closer, but I only had the strength to reach out for his fingers. That elicited another laugh from him.

"You want to eat?" he asked, pulling out some sandwiches from his bag.

"Mmmm," I hesitated. I wasn't sure what eating would do to my stomach at the moment. I decided on the sandwiches. I'd much rather have eaten and end up vomiting than do more of that on an empty stomach.

It turned out to be the right choice, for I began to feel better almost immediately. The rushing of blood in my ears gave way to the musical trickle of the stream. The burn of protesting muscles faded, leaving a warm, not unpleasant ache. And the sickening loathing I felt for Lucas disappeared in the overwhelming brightness of the love I felt for Cale, and he for me. Right then, the whole world could have ceased to exist, and I don't think I would have noticed.

"I do feel safe," I said to Cale. "Like you said. No one can touch us."

"You are, you know," he replied, gathering me close against him. "He won't dare cross a line I've set for him."

"What about me, though?" I asked, confused by the complexities of this situation. "Didn't I put myself inside of his territory, when I ..."

"There is nothing outside of my reach, if that's what you mean."

"Come to think of it, actually, if that's true, then how come he could get to me in the first place? He came right into my garden. Didn't you protect me from him then?"

Cale breathed a heavy sigh, and I sat up, looking down at him. "Didn't you?" I repeated.

"I did," he said. "I protected you every way I could. And he couldn't get to you, not at first."

"Then how?" I demanded.

"He talked to me," he said simply. My eyes went wide. I began to see where this was going, but I didn't want to believe it. "He made an argument I couldn't deny."

I got up and began to pace. Cale sat up and spoke in a soothing tone. "He knew about you—because he had seen you in that blasted clearing, near the border of Iffreyn. So he taunted me, told me you didn't really love me."

That stopped me. I couldn't bear to meet Cale's eyes, so I looked down at the rock, tracing the fissures in the stone with my eyes.

"I told him you did, and I'd stake my life on it." The conviction in his voice told me he still meant that, even after all I had done. "He told me I had forced you to love me, since you didn't know anything else. He asked me to let him talk to you, and see if you still loved me after he was done. Then, and only then, he said, would I know for sure."

I shuddered. "So you tested me?"

"Yes, in a way, and no. I gave you your freedom."

"Freedom," I said with a bitter laugh. "What kind of freedom that turned out to be! I know a little better what real freedom is, now." I turned to him at last, forlorn. "But I failed your test. Why would you still come back for me if you know now that I didn't love you like you thought I did?"

"I knew the way you loved me." His voice was steady, but his eyes were far away.

"You knew? You knew I would fail?" His expression was all the answer I needed. "Then why would you let me do that to you?"

He stood up from the rock and came to hold my face in his hands. "Don't you know that yet?" he said. "*I* love *you*. There is no test you can try that will show you otherwise. I could not love you perfectly if I didn't give you a chance to have whatever freedom you wanted. And I came back to find you for the same reason. I love you, and I knew you wanted me to save you."

"Oh, Cale," I sobbed. "I love you, I love you, I love you! You must know that now. Even when I betrayed you, I still loved you. But it wasn't enough."

"Then let my love be enough," he said, "And let me worry about how much love I need from you." He held both my hands to his lips.

We went back to practicing, but this time it wasn't Lucas's face I saw. It wasn't my betrayal that hounded me to greater and greater feats of strength. It was Cale and only Cale I knew as I twirled and slashed, stabbed and leaped on the sunny bank of the stream. It was his love that spurred me on, his presence beside me that flooded my aching muscles with strength.

—

Dinner was an ordeal that night, though I couldn't begrudge the smirks and quiet snorts of not–quite–laughter around the table. Mike and Gabe were particularly amused by my feeble attempts at feeding myself. It didn't help that we were eating steak, and no matter how tender the meat nor how sharp the knife, I couldn't seem to get through it. Cale whispered an offer of help, but I shook my head, renewing my efforts with stiff–necked pride. But when my steak shot off my plate and into my lap, I accepted Cale's offer, adding my laughter to their helpless guffaws.

When I had eaten my fill—which was a lot after today's hard work and fresh air—I begged excuse and took my dishes to the sink. Even that was difficult, my wrist burning as I walked with quicker and quicker steps, almost dropping the plate into the soapy water. As I passed by the table, Mike gave me a playful clap on the shoulder that made me wince.

"Gee, thanks," I said, scowling. Cale rose and kissed me as I passed him.

"Sleep well, sweet," he said with a smile. "Tomorrow we do it again."

I groaned. Annie rose and laid a worn hand on my back.

"Emma, I've got something that might help you. Boys, you'll see to the washing up?" Mike and Gabe clambered off their chairs, looking like two bears on doll's furniture, and headed to the sink as Annie led me upstairs.

"Epsom salts," she said, rummaging in a bathroom cupboard and coming out with her prize. "That's the thing for you. Here, now." She bustled away to my room and into my bathroom, turning the water on full and sprinkling a good cup–full of salts into the bottom of the tub. She rolled up one sleeve, bent over and reached into the deep tub, swirling the water with her hand to dissolve the minerals. They were scented—a steaming bloom of soft floral aroma filled the air, bringing to mind a rich meadow of Otherworld.

"Thank you," I said. I felt badly just watching her run my bath for me, but she had such a graceful, efficient way about her that I couldn't match. Besides, she probably wouldn't want me interfering anyway, based on what I knew about her.

"It's nothing," she said. "I'm just so glad to have you here at last. It is good to see Cale so happy."

"You've known Cale a long time?" I was curious about these friends.

"As long as anyone can," she replied with a knowing smile.

"Then you are from Otherworld? You are immortal...like me?"

"Yes. We came long ago, at Cale's request. We, and others like us, have been watching over you."

"Me?" I asked, startled. "I had no idea."

"You didn't think Cale would simply leave you alone, did you?" she chided.

I sputtered. "Well, I didn't really know what I thought. I didn't remember anything."

"I know, poor child," Annie sighed. "It was awful seeing you like that. I know it broke Cale's heart for so long."

"He was watching me, too?" I asked, astounded by these new revelations.

"Constantly. Most of the time he kept his distance, waiting. He tried, other times, you know."

"Tried what?" I breathed, though by the quickening of my

heart, I seemed to know the answer already.

"He tried to woo you. You wouldn't...you weren't ready, I guess."

I looked away, searching through the jumbled memories of my centuries with Lucas. It was hard, for I shied away from anything that might cause me pain like last night. But as I concentrated and scanned through the millions of faces that filed through my long, disjointed life, I found him—a stranger under a lamppost. It was a theme repeated in a hundred variations—in a chariot in ancient Rome, by a bar in a sailors' brothel, at the Paris Opera, in a fish market by the sea, at the foot of an Aztec temple, in a Chicago speakeasy...and the constant was his persistent love, and my cautious curiosity. But there was always the rebuff, the laugh, the call for Lucas's lackeys to chase him off, once even a slap across the face, and always watching the stranger walk away alone. Until now.

I came out of the memories with an incoherent cry.

"He never said anything!" I said, distraught. "He came, so many times. How could he keep coming, when I treated him like that?"

"Simple, m'girl," Annie smiled. "He loves you."

"But why?" I breathed in wonder, turning to look at myself in the mirror. What possible attraction could I command, that he would endure ages of scorn for the chance that I might one day say yes?

"I could venture a few ideas, but you'd have to ask him, to be sure," Annie said with a smile. "Now, enjoy your bath, Princess. I've left a salve for your aches on the vanity."

When she left, I glanced once more at the mirror, searching the wide blue eyes that met me there, then smiling as my reflection and I shared the wonderful knowledge of Cale's love.

—

"Why do you love me?" I asked Cale point blank.

"Well, good morning to you, too," he said with a charming smile, taking me into his arms. I looked up at him with my best I–mean–business expression.

"Haven't I answered that already?" he asked, cocking one eyebrow.

I shook my head. "Not satisfactorily."

"No? Well, I suppose it wouldn't satisfy you if I just said 'because'?"

I swatted at him, then instantly regretted it as my muscles protested. I winced.

"If you're sore today," Cale said with a glint of mischief in his eye, "Then imagine how much worse it'll be tomorrow!"

I groaned, slumping theatrically in his arms.

"Come on, lazybones," he said, strapping my sword around my waist the way he wore his. He took my hand in his, lifting the picnic basket with the other, and we set off in the soft dawn light.

"You didn't answer my question," I reminded him as we walked away from the back door of the manor.

"That's because words aren't enough, my Emma. I could tell you it's because you're breathtakingly beautiful, astoundingly clever and talented, and strong and sweet and wonderful and everything else I could possibly want. Mostly it's just because I like the way I feel when I'm with you. But I get the feeling that's still not enough for you."

I shrugged. "It's a start." I laughed. "Really? Breathtakingly beautiful?"

"Mm–hm!" he said with an emphatic nod.

"I can believe that I was once. Are you sure you're not just remembering the way I used to be?"

"Emma," he said, stopping to get my attention. "You are beautiful to me no matter what. You could be wearing a potato sack with your head shaved and you couldn't fool me, not for a second."

I laughed, warmed by his words. His presence seemed to chase away the lingering doubts, like the morning sun chased the mist from the pasture.

"Now, come on, and let's get practicing." He pulled me along.

"Cale?"

"Yes?" he glanced at me as he helped me over a stile into a flower–rich meadow.

"Annie told me—that you've tried before. That you've been watching over me."

"And?" He didn't look at my face. He seemed to be holding his breath as he waited.

"I'm sorry. I'll never be able to say it enough."

He looked at me then, holding out his hand to stroke my cheek. "I wasn't looking for an apology. I wondered if you'd be angry with me for not succeeding sooner." He sighed. "Emma, I didn't rescue you so you could wallow in self-loathing for the rest of your life. I just wanted you back. I wanted you to be with me. I wanted you to want me."

"I do!" I avowed, kissing him in demonstration. He kissed me back fervently, then put me away from him.

"Now, enough of this sorry business. Let's get back to

work." He started on the way again, but I hung back.

"Cale?" I asked hesitantly. "Can I say something?"

"As long as it's not sorry again," he said with a laugh.

"Is it okay to say thank you?" I ventured.

He smiled. "As much as you like."

I put my hand in his and followed him.

"Thank you," I said, leaning my head against his shoulder. "Thank you, thank you, thank you."

7

"**I** want you to look at something," Cale said. The way he raised his eyebrows suggested to me that he was worried about the way I would react. It had been a long morning session, and I was often grouchy when I was tired.

"What is it?" I asked, putting down my water bottle and peering at him. He pulled something out of his pocket—something vaguely familiar as if from another lifetime. He held it out to me, a small oblong that was cold and hard in my hand. I looked at it. The mirror.

I remembered this thing, and my reaction to it the first time Cale had shown it to me. I took a deep breath, holding it at arm's length. I wouldn't look at it lightly this time.

"Go ahead," Cale said with a little smile. "Trust me."

I made a show of looking at it with one eye, then in spite of myself, I opened the other eye and examined it closely.

My outward reflection had changed greatly over the past few weeks. My frame had both filled out and grown lean as good food put meat on my bones, and heavy exercise corded it into muscle. My face was fuller, but not soft. As my training had hardened my body, it had also made muscular angles in my face. My hair had grown somewhat, and I'd let it go wavy without access to a flat iron. It was also back to my real strawberry blonde colour, after a box of hair dye had mysteriously shown up on my bathroom vanity. I suspected Annie. Even without makeup, my skin had a healthy rose glow, and the dark smudges under my eyes were gone.

Almost immediately, the Otherworldly images flickered across the mirror—the way I saw myself, and the way I truly was. The latter was less of a surprise, now that I had my memory back. The long flowing hair, the starry crown, the white dress, the sweet innocence of my face—that was the way I remembered myself, once, and so was more familiar. I looked at it with wistful longing, wishing I could be like that for Cale once again, and knowing it wasn't possible.

It was the third reflection, the way I saw myself that was the most changed. I remembered the image I had seen the first time, when I'd dropped the mirror, with fear for what I might see this time. I realized that on my first glance it was not my own perception that had caused me to drop the mirror, but the way Cale saw me. The starveling wretch I had expected, somewhere in my subconscious. But the Princess was beyond my wildest dreams.

This time I saw something else entirely. It was not quite as good as I really looked, and fell far short of my "true" self, but it was a lot closer. Although I still saw myself as slightly disfigured and malnourished, there was a spark of hope in my eyes and a faint bloom of colour in my cheeks. My hair was brighter and softer, and I actually smiled at myself.

I looked up at Cale in wonder. He smiled encouragingly at me.

"You know what I see," he said. "Now you are starting to change the way you see yourself."

I glanced back at the mirror as if to reassure myself that the reflection was still the same. Then I extended it to Cale.

"Keep it," he said, pushing it back towards me and curling my fingers around it. "It was meant for you in the first place."

"Thank you," I whispered, holding it against my heart.

"This way you can always be reminded of who you really are."

"But you'll be here to remind me," I prompted. When he answered with a grunt and turned away, my heart jumped in alarm. But something about his posture made me hesitant to ask him about it.

"There's something else you need to learn now," he said. "We'll keep working with the sword, but you're going to have to know how to begin weaving this world back together with Otherworld."

My pulse quickened. This was what I was made for, my home, Cale's kingdom. Every connection, every bridge we built between this world and the other was one step closer to the day that Cale and I could be together again in our palace. I closed my eyes to savour the memories of our times together riding the valley on horseback, walking the alpine meadows full of flowers, standing at the battlements together in the sunset. There was nothing I wouldn't give to get that back again.

"How do we do that?" I asked.

"Love," Cale said simply.

"What?"

"Love."

"That's it?" I asked, not sure I understood.

"Yep," he replied. "Love. Random acts of kindness, for starters. Do you remember the waitress in that diner, when we went on our first date?"

"If you could call it a date," I said wryly. I almost said

sorry again, but the look on Cale's face stopped me. Yes, I remembered the waitress, and the way he had given her exactly what she'd needed—not just money, but the words that had set her free. "I thought you were out of your mind, if I recall correctly. So that's what you're talking about?"

"Yeah. That's one thing. It's different for every person you meet. But it all comes down to the one concept."

"Love," I mused. "Huh."

"When *he* took you, he ruined everything he could. The best way he could do that was through fear."

"Fear, hmmm? I can see that." I could see it very clearly. Lucas had kept me a prisoner in fear for thousands of years.

"For each person, there is a different way to release them from that fear."

"How will I know?" I asked. This seemed a daunting task, knowing as well as I did how powerful Lucas could be.

"I'll help you to know," Cale said, rubbing my upper arm in reassurance. "You'll come with me tomorrow, into town, and I'll show you what I mean."

"Love," I said aloud again, shaking my head. "All you need is love ..." I sang softly, and Cale laughed.

"Yeah."

—

Sedgebury was a pretty, anytown kind of place, nestled in a sheltered valley not too far from Simon and Annie's estate. As we drove onto the main street, I wondered if there was much need for Cale's work here—at first glance it seemed so picturesque and peaceful that I didn't imagine love was something they lacked.

We went into a corner diner, the kind of country family

restaurant you see in the movies, with wood panelling and up-holstered booths. It struck me as odd, though I didn't realize why at the time, that the restaurant was quite full of people, especially men. Cale, Mike, Gabe and I seated ourselves in a booth where we could command a good view of the rest of the diner.

Cale picked up a menu. "What do you see, Emma?" he asked, not looking up from his perusal.

I was mildly surprised at the way he jumped into things, but I was up to the challenge. I squared my shoulders, settled myself, and began to scan the room. I let my eyes pass over each person on the first go, then took a little more time on the next. There really were a lot of men here, and when I saw the time on the clock, I understood why. 10:30 in the morning. Too late for breakfast, too early for lunch. Most people would be at work right now, aside from the odd senior citizen or stay–at–home mother.

That was when I began to notice things—the want ads in the newspapers, many with a great deal of circles, many of the circles crossed out, the tense lines between the men's eye-brows, the hunch to their shoulders, the furtive, fearful glanc-es the waitresses gave the men as they refilled their coffee cups, the flush of embarrassment on a woman's face as her debit card was rejected.

"Something's going on, here," I murmured, intrigued. "A lot of people are unemployed. It seems to be affecting the whole town." I shot a look at Cale. "I'm way off base, aren't I?"

"No," he said, putting down his menu. "You're exactly right. The local textile factory closed down three months ago and there are no jobs to be had. You've hit on the most obvious problem. But there is more to this."

"More?" I asked, looking again. I did feel it, but I couldn't put my finger on what it was.

"Use your mirror," Cale said, pinning me with a significant stare. At first I didn't know what he was talking about. But then I remembered the cold oblong in my pocket. The mirror of truth. I pulled it out and looked at myself as if to check my lipstick. But when I tilted it to view the space behind and beside me, I froze. I nearly screamed.

When I saw the scene with my own eyes, I saw a man at the table, resting his head in one hand with his hair all spiked up from his worrying fingers, and his other hand holding a sharpie to circle ads. But the mirror told a different story. In the mirror, I still saw the man, but there was a second figure behind him.

The figure there didn't belong in this homely setting. He was like something out of ancient history, or out of a Tolkein book. He was armed to the teeth and frighteningly fierce, dressed in armour and livery of deep crimson and black, with a familiar symbol on the front that chilled my blood. His hand rested oppressively on the back of the oblivious man's neck, and he looked directly at me in the mirror with a haughty sneer.

My heartbeat raced and I was in serious danger of hyperventilating, but Cale put his arm around me and I felt much better.

"Is he...is he really here?" I breathed, not taking my eyes off the mirror.

"Yes," Cale said simply.

I felt like I might throw up. Lucas's men had found me

here! It was only a matter of minutes before he confronted Cale to take me back. Was this it, now? No, surely not one man alone against three.

"How many more are there? How many times have they been with me and I didn't know it?"

"They are just about everywhere," Cale said. "But they won't hang around if I won't let them."

As I watched the invisible minion in the mirror, I saw his eyes flicker to Cale. I didn't miss the moment of intense loathing and fear that flashed through his eyes. That surprised me. But I suppose it shouldn't have. I knew, after all, that Lucas and his army had never dared cross into Cale's kingdom, even from the beginning. Never, that is, until I gave him a reason.

I felt a familiar twinge of guilt, and I had the unsettling experience of watching my estimation of myself drop in the mirror. The thug must have caught my lapse, for he looked back at me and smiled evilly. But then I saw myself as Cale did, and I glared back. I was a Princess, now a warrior, and I wouldn't let myself be cowed by this Otherworld monster.

"What do we do?" I asked Cale.

"Ask him to leave."

I favoured Cale with an incredulous expression. "And if he doesn't?"

"Give him my name. He'll go."

"Okay," I said dubiously. I looked at him in the mirror, straight into his horrifying eyes, and said. "Cale says to go."

With a snarl of defeat that I couldn't hear, he dissolved in a jumble of red angles, which dissipated like red smoke. In the centre of the mist, a white light flickered and grew, forming a tracery of interlacing lines, like Cale's symbol. For a moment,

I caught a glimpse of a verdant meadow, and heard the faint sound of a brook as though borne from a distance on a breeze.

The man at the table sighed, and his shoulders seemed to relax a little. He would only think that his mood had lightened, maybe that the coffee he had just drunk had kicked in. But I knew differently. A heavy hand had lifted from his neck. He was free...more or less.

"That's not it, is it?" I said. "There's something more we have to do."

Cale nodded, his eyes smiling slightly at my perceptiveness.

"He still doesn't have a job." I fluffed at my hair as I pondered the situation. Well, the immediate need was money. It was for everyone in the room. But that was something I didn't have.

"I wish there was something I could do," I said, watching helplessly.

"There is," Cale murmured, putting a bill in my hand.

The waitress was coming just now. My heart pounded, knowing the significance of what I was about to do. She began pouring coffee.

"Excuse me," I said, and her eyes met mine, startled. "Do you see that man over there? Could you take this, and pay for anything he orders?" I gave her the wadded–up bill, which she unfolded with a look of shock.

"This is a hundred," she said, holding the bill out as if to give it back. "It's too much."

"No," I said, glancing at Cale. "Start up a tab for him. Tell him he can have whatever he wants, until it's gone."

"And if he asks who to thank?" She raised an eyebrow,

looking at me suspiciously.

I looked at Cale, and he smiled back proudly, with his eyebrows cocked as if to say, what are you going to do next?

"Tell him it was compliments of Cale Kynsey."

The waitress left, and we rose to leave before the man knew. I noticed Cale left a large tip for the waitress. As we opened the door, I looked back over my shoulder to see the waitress talking to the man. His face was singular as he went from confusion, to blank shock, to amazed gratitude.

I took Cale's arm and leaned my head against his shoulder. It was a small thing, but it was one more step towards finding Otherworld here again.

—

I walked the halls of Simon and Annie's home that night, my mind full of thoughts. The events in the diner had awakened me to a whole new realm I hadn't known existed. On the one hand, Lucas's agents were all around. That was a sobering thought. But I knew how to defeat them, now, and I had no fear that with Cale beside me, I was invincible.

On the other hand, I saw the needs of others in a whole new light. While Lucas held me under the thrall of Ambrosia, I had cared only for myself, and even that very little. It was as though I had been frozen and numb, and I was only now beginning to thaw out. Cale and I had helped one person today, but there were so many others in that restaurant that still needed help. I found I cared very much about those people, and not just as a means to the end of rejoining Otherworld. I wondered if they felt as trapped as I had before Cale had freed me.

My mind kept circling back to the people in the diner. I

knew the key was love. I had seen it work. But on a large scale? The town's problem seemed insurmountable, at least for one person. What could I possibly do, even with Cale's help, to fix all the wrongs that I had made happen?

I came to a gallery overlooking the main hall. Hanging there on the wall was a beautiful tapestry, depicting a stag pursued by a hunter in full armour, mounted on a horse with his lady behind him, against a backdrop of trees. It hung from floor to vaulted ceiling, woven out of dense and smoothly spun wool. I reached out to brush my fingers over the surface. It looked almost new.

"I made that when I first came from Otherworld to this place," Annie said just behind me.

I whirled, putting my hands behind my back.

"Oh, go ahead," she said kindly, coming over to stroke the tapestry, running her fingers tenderly over warp and weft. "It can take it."

"It's beautiful."

"Thank you. It's a gift, you know. From *him*."

"Cale? I thought you said ..."

"Oh, I did make it. What I mean is that all beautiful things are a gift from the Prince. All the talents we are given, every stirring song or poem, every meaningful painting, every delightful vista or perfect bloom—it is all a reminder of the place we belong. It's all for you."

"Me?" I asked, startled. I took a second look at the tapestry. I couldn't put my finger on it, but I had the sudden feeling as though every stitch of the tapestry was a message of love, direct from Cale to me. I touched the fabric reverently, wondering how many times I had seen one of his love-notes in a sunset or heard his sweet nothings in a song on the radio and been unaware.

"I wish the rheumatism wasn't so bad, or I'd still be making them. I never had such problems in Otherworld. My mind is brimming over with pictures." She waved her hand around her head in demonstration and smiled wistfully, and I had the feeling her hands were itching to hold a weaving shuttle again.

I sighed. So much wrong with the world. Why couldn't Annie be young forever in her rightful home, able to use her talent for weaving? Why couldn't the people in town have a livelihood? Why couldn't the world be free from the oppression of Lucas and his agents? I knew the answer to that, and I closed my eyes against the pain of my guilt.

But when I closed my eyes I saw Cale's face. He had come back for me. He would make it all okay again. I opened my eyes with new purpose.

"He loves you so much, you know," Annie said, watching my face.

"I know." I breathed deeply, dragging that knowledge down to my toes.

Annie patted my cheek. "Don't let it all get to you, dear. Just remember what's important."

She left me alone with my thoughts by the tapestry, leaning back against the gallery railing. I thought about all the pictures in Annie's head that would never become tapestries. I thought about the closed textile mill just outside of the town. I thought of the flocks of sheep that dotted the country hillsides, and just then the pieces came together like a puzzle.

Only one piece was missing, and I would have to keep my eyes open if I wanted to find it.

—

"Where are we going?" I asked, following Cale along the overgrown path. We seemed to be entering a solid tunnel of green, so dense were the thickets on either side. Birds sang out all around us, and the wind picked up a chorus from the millions of leaves.

"You'll see," he said, forging on through the bracken. "I won't steer you wrong."

"Never thought you would," I said with a smile.

He let out a single laugh that suggested disbelief.

"I mean, now I don't."

He turned in the shelter of the forest, taking me in his arms. "That's behind us now. I didn't mean to remind you."

"It's okay," I shook away the rising tears, for once successful. He kissed my forehead and let go of me, his hand taking my fingers loosely.

"Come on, then."

We walked hand in hand through the forest tunnel, and for an endless moment I felt as though I might have been back in Otherworld, but for the occasional bother of biting insects. At last I could see a circle of golden light ahead, and we emerged into a sun-drenched meadow spotted with cloud shadows. After the cool, deep shade of the wood, the colours of the scene burst across my senses—the vivid green of the field and the saturated blue of the sky between white, gold, and indigo clouds.

Ahead of us was a steep, sweeping hill, with a castle at the top. I had thought that Avenham was grand, but this was far beyond anything I'd seen in a long time. It was a smallish castle, compact and tall, but it was undeniably old and beyond price, with its time–blackened stone and carved white ramparts. Still, the place had a closed–in air about it, so different from the welcoming atmosphere of Simon and Annie's home.

I went to step forward, but Cale put his hand out to stop me. He took out the big canvas pack he carried our swords in for practice, unzipped it, and passed me my sword. I looked at it for a moment, uncomprehending.

"We're going to walk up to this castle with *swords*?"

"Drawn, preferably," he said grimly, his eyes focussed on the tall gate of the castle. Something in his eyes triggered my adrenaline, and belatedly I pulled my mirror out of my pocket. A quick glance confirmed what my reflexes already knew. Two of Lucas's thugs stood as sentinels by the door.

I didn't hesitate then to draw my sword.

"Won't whoever lives here see our swords and wonder?" I asked. "I mean, they don't exactly know there are warriors camped outside their door."

He smiled. "No, they won't wonder. They won't even see. These are Otherworldly blades, my Emma." He swung his sword in an arc that caught the sunlight with a brilliant flash. "Rare is the person who marks the passing of an Otherworld battle. It happens all the time without anyone taking notice."

I stared at him with wild eyes.

"Don't worry," he said, stroking my cheek briefly. "Stay behind me. They won't dare cause you harm."

"Then why do I need the sword?" I asked sceptically.

He laughed, then sobered as he began to stride purposefully towards the castle. I tagged along, feeling very much out of my depth. As we rounded the top of the hill, Cale looked around, presumably to be sure there were no hidden men lurking to the sides or behind us.

"Just the two by the door?" I asked.

He nodded. "Lucas knows it's not likely anyone, besides me, is going to attack this stronghold. If anyone did, he wouldn't need more than two to hold the gate. And he knows that if I come, no amount of guards could hold me back."

I glanced up at his profile, slightly winded from the climb, but more so breathless from his magnificence. His words might have sounded egotistical coming from a lesser man. But from him, I could believe that he meant it, and deserved it, nothing beyond that.

The guards at the door certainly looked like they would confirm Cale's reputation. They had spotted us long before, and I had been checking my mirror as frequently as I could while still maintaining my balance on the uneven ground. But I hoped it wouldn't come down to me having to fight, because I couldn't imagine how I'd strike a moving target I couldn't see with a sword I had just learned to use.

When we were unbearably close to the door, Cale nudged me behind him, raising his sword before him.

"Be gone!" he shouted. I watched in my mirror, upside down. It was unnerving to see their mouths move and not hear their response.

Whatever they said made Cale crouch into an offensive pose. I held my breath for an agonizing moment. But the dread guards broke formation and vanished. Cale wasted no time in closing the ground he'd won and opening the heavy, tall door.

The place inside was dark and oppressive. Even the beams of sunlight that came through the narrow windows of the gate room gave a feeble watery light and petered out within a foot or two. The air was close, unmoved, and smelled of damp stone and old wood. Everything about the room reminded me of something else, long ago—a dark and twisted forest where nothing stirred and even the light was banished.

The door swung shut behind me, off–balance on its hinges, and I fought to keep my breath under control. Every instinct in my body told me to run. I must have made some sort of half–strangled sound, for Cale reached back and squeezed my hand.

"Hello?" he called out. The gesture was needless, though, for he knew where he was going. He moved along the wall to the right and into a long, tall corridor that was only slightly better lit. On the right was a high wall with narrow windows set in the upper half. On the left, several closed doors lined the lower story, while a balcony ran the length of the upper floor. Cale headed unerringly to the end of the corridor and turned left.

There was a TV on somewhere near—I could hear the vibrations in the air even before I could see the blue light flickering under the door. I checked my mirror again, and the hallway was clear. But I was not naïve enough to think that Lucas didn't have more henchmen here.

Cale approached the door, sword drawn and ready. As he approached, the door flung open of its own accord, as if from a sudden, powerful gust of wind, though the air in the place was still. Cale tensed, ready to spring.

Then, acting on a cue I neither heard nor saw, Cale slashed out with his sword, faster than I had ever seen him move. He whirled and hacked, lunged and stabbed. I held my sword up, though I wouldn't know what to strike at if it came down to it.

I watched in awe as he rained down frenzied blows on invisible foes.

"Submit and be gone!" he shouted, setting an echo spinning through the vaulted corridor. He stopped fighting, waiting with a wary stance. Then the guards must have disappeared, for he stood upright and sheathed his sword.

"They're gone," he said grimly, walking toward the open door.

"How many were there?" I asked, still in awe.

"Six," he said nonchalantly, as if it was a matter of course to beat down six armed opponents at once unaided. He strode through the door and looked around.

I followed, getting my own impression of the room. It had evidently once been very beautiful, though time and neglect had taken some of the sheen from the polished oak panelling and dust had settled on the priceless furniture. The room was stuffed with antiquities and rarities, each one unimaginably valuable.

A lone leather wingback chair stood in the centre of the room, angled towards an old but large television that filled the dim room with flickering, unearthly light. Someone sat in the chair, quite still, with his trousered legs and slippered feet propped up on a footstool, and one arm laid over the arm of the chair and a curled hand resting on a small round table beside a mug and an empty plate. I didn't need to check my mirror to know that the room was now empty, but for us and the castle's owner.

"Hello there," Cale called out, his voice as steady as if he'd been perfectly relaxed, rather than fighting off a mob of Otherworld enemies.

"Oh, hello," came a voice from the wing chair, and a face turned to see us. "I didn't know anyone was here." The old man tried to get up, but Cale waved him back.

"No, no," he said. "Don't get up on our account. We've just come to see how you're doing."

"Oh, that was kind," the man said. "Nobody bothers to come see me very often anymore. But do you know, I'm feeling much better today." He paused and rubbed his back thoughtfully. "I hadn't noticed. Hurt like the devil this morning, but now...hmmm." He had a puzzled look on his face. I glanced at Cale, who smiled meaningfully at me.

"I don't believe I'm acquainted with you folks," the old man continued. "Though these days I forget everything. Sometimes I think I'll forget my own name!"

Cale laughed. "My name is Cale Kynsey, and this is Emma Delaney. We are friends of Simon and Annie, who live just beyond the wood at Avenham."

"Oh, yes, I remember Simon and Annie," he said with a surprised smile. "They're still alive? They're even older than I," he added, with a wink at me. "My name is Solomon Hatch. It's a pleasure to meet you both."

We entered into an unexpectedly gratifying conversation. He offered us refreshments, but I suggested I could fetch them instead. It took some time to light the ancient gas stove and wait for the iron kettle to boil. Even more to find the tea cups, which were housed in a small room devoted to the china. I chose the set that looked the least valuable, in fear that I might break them. I found some biscuits and placed the whole arrangement on a tea cart. When I returned, Solomon was speaking of the castle and its history, even at one point implying a dark past there. At once, both Cale and I were interested.

"Do you mean it's haunted?" I asked, looking up as I unloaded the contents of the trolley onto the little table. I exchanged a meaningful look with Cale.

"You might call it that," he mused. "Some have given it that name, in the past. Strange happenings and all that. But I've never seen anything myself. Only felt a sense of unease. It could just be the vain imaginings of an old man." He waved his hand dismissively. "But some have spoken of a family curse. It's true, though the Hatch family has never lacked for wealth, we have suffered more than our fair share of misfortune.

"There's my own father—lost a leg in an accident. My mother left him and three small children. My two sisters both died of the same disease that weakened me. Then there's my Granny who went insane as a young woman one day, just as if someone had thrown a switch—she never did speak again after that. There's plenty of other stories, too. People got the idea that Sedgebury Castle is cursed or haunted, and pretty soon they stopped visiting us. They leave me alone most of the time, and I'm ashamed to say, with all the pain I'm in most days, I can be a crotchety old soul, so I'm certain I chase them away as much as the curse."

I glanced at Cale again, though he didn't look back at me this time.

"I'm sorry for all the trouble you've had," he said, his eyes filled with genuine compassion. "I hope there is some way to make it right."

"Well, it certainly is nice to have a visit from some nice young people like you."

"The pleasure is ours," I said.

"You two seem to be quite friendly," Solomon said, changing the subject as he looked shrewdly from Cale to me. "Take my advice, young man," he turned toward Cale, "A girl like that doesn't come along every day. I should know. Snap her up before someone else does."

"I've been working on that," Cale said with a smile as he reached for my hand. I looked down, blushing. He neglected to mention he'd been working on that for thousands of years. But at last, at last I was in my right mind.

We took our leave well before dinner, with a promise we'd send someone with a basket of goodies for him. He looked so frail, I hated to leave him to fend for himself.

"We'll be back again soon, I promise," I said when we took our leave.

His eyes smiled, though he mock pouted for our benefit.

As we walked down the hallway and out through the massive gates, I tried to put Cale's battle out of my mind. But I didn't quite succeed.

"Were they the problem? Lucas's soldiers?" I asked.

Cale nodded.

"Will he be okay now?"

He nodded again, this time with a confident smile.

"You know what?" I asked rhetorically. "I love you."

"I love you, too," he said, pulling me under his arm and kissing the top of my head.

—

As promised, we went up to Sedgebury Castle the very next day with a basket of fresh baked treats and jams from Annie's kitchen. We found Solomon on the way, crossing the meadow with a walking stick in hand, the tip of the twisted length of wood barely kissing the ground as he walked.

I watched him approach in astonishment. Yesterday he could barely rise from his chair. I glanced at Cale, and he smiled back with satisfaction. Taking my hand, he ran with me to meet up with our new friend.

"I thought you couldn't walk," I said delightedly.

"So did I," he answered with a jovial smile. Already his cheeks looked pinker, less waxy. His eyes sparkled, not with the wasted glassy gleam of an invalid, but with the bright joy of someone fully alive. "But ever since you came to visit me, I have felt better and better by the moment. I swear I haven't felt this fit since I was a boy! I feel certain you have restored me."

He looked at Cale as though searching for any sort of admission of this feat, but Cale merely looked at him steadily, as he had me when we had first met. I still felt like squirming, sometimes, under that unflinchingly honest gaze. I saw some kind of elemental comprehension dawn in Solomon's eyes, as though his heart knew what his head might never piece together.

"I feel certain I could never repay what you've done for me," he said, his jocular voice now subdued. "But everything I have is at your disposal—the castle, my fortune, my life!" He gave a little laugh. Then to our surprise, he grabbed us both up in a vigorous hug that would have been impossible for him before today.

"Now, take me to your Simon and Annie, and we shall have a visit."

As we walked back to the estate, thoughts began to spin in my head, like a web joining bright points of light. There was the ailing town, the empty factory, the experienced but idle workers, the sheep, the tapestry, a head full of ideas...and a fortune at Cale's disposal...I hardly dared dream it was coming together like this, but when I looked at Cale, I saw him wink at me. It was all I needed to embolden me.

"Do you know, Mr. Hatch," I said, hooking my hand into his elbow, "There might be some way to use that fortune for good, and save the town at the same time."

"I'm all ears, my dear," he said.

———

Summer bloomed to full flush, and began to decline before we had it all worked out. But by the beginning of September, we had the makings of a new tapestry factory, complete with funding, design department, management, and workers. I had the joy of turning all the kudos to Cale whenever anyone thanked me.

We spent most of our time, when we weren't working on the factory, training in the clearing and seeking out any last vestiges of Lucas's power in the town. I never ceased to be amazed by Cale's prowess as a warrior, even if no one else could see it. He was incredible! I couldn't imagine anything, not even Lucas, standing up against him.

As for me, I flourished in the countryside, in Cale's company. Here, at his side, I was respectable. I was important again. I was clean and lovely and I felt like I fit with him. When I looked in my mirror, I began to see the three images grow closer and closer to each other until my perception of myself and my physical appearance began to match my true self almost exactly.

I couldn't really remember who I had been, or perhaps I didn't let myself. Even in those moments when I was alone and I let my mind wander to those darker days, I couldn't reconcile the wretch that I had been with who I was now, and who I had begun. It was almost as if those centuries apart from Cale hadn't even happened. I felt as if Lucas no longer had the power to touch me.

Until one evening. We were gathered around the kitchen table, after a long day of planning the factory and training for battle.

"We'll be going back to the city next week," Cale blurted out.

Simon, Annie, Gabe, and Mike all absorbed this easily, as if they had expected it. Perhaps I had expected it, as well. But I was anything but easy about it. My mind was cast into an instant maelstrom of conflicted feelings. On the one hand, I wanted this to be over—a final confrontation that would take Lucas out of our lives forever and restore everything to the way it should be. After all, then we could be married that much sooner.

But when I thought about being near to Lucas again, I was very, very afraid. Not afraid for Cale, or for my own safety. I was afraid that all the strength I had built, all the knowledge I had gained, all the love Cale had lavished on me would be for nothing. I was afraid I would fail, again.

8

Packing was simple—I had never had much to hold on to since Lucas had stolen me away. I took my time folding up the clothes that Cale had bought for me before his gallant rescue mission. There were a few toiletries: a toothbrush and toothpaste, deodorant, shampoo, conditioner, soap, a brush, some moisturizer and a lip gloss. I packed them carefully to avoid spilling anything nasty. I wouldn't pack my sword and my mirror away—those I would keep on me at all times.

Then I spent a few moments looking around the lavish apartments where I had spent the past months. The beautiful but comfortable rooms had become the only real home to me in the millennia since leaving Cale's palace. I felt an unexpected pang of loss as I thought of leaving this place that was as close to Otherworld as I might get for now. I would miss Simon and Annie terribly.

When I could stall no longer, I picked up my light suitcase and with a backward glance, left my rooms behind. Everyone was waiting at the foot of the stairs. Annie had a basket with sandwiches in waxed paper and fruit and cheese and a condensation–covered bottle of lemonade. She handed this to me and in one motion wrapped me up in a bony but strong hug. Simon was next to embrace me.

It was then that I noticed there was only one suitcase besides mine. Cale had his bag at his feet, but Mike and Gabe had none. As Gabe moved in to hug me goodbye, I froze, confused.

"What's going on?" I asked. "Aren't you guys coming, too?"

"Cale wants you two to go alone," Mike said, casting a glance at his Prince that didn't quite mask all of his apprehension. My confidence about our trip to the city dropped a few notches.

"Shouldn't they come, too?" I implored Cale, my eyes wide.

Cale didn't answer. Instead, it was Gabe. "If Cale doesn't want us to come, then there is a reason. He knows what he is doing."

"Oh, well in that case ..." I said cheerfully, but still not convinced. I swung the picnic basket playfully and looked back over my shoulder. "What are we waiting for?"

We walked down the steps to the car, where there was another round of hugs before we got in, closed the doors, and drove away. I watched our friends recede into the distance, my heart quickening at the thought of being alone with Cale—alone against the wiles of Lucas.

I had full confidence in Cale. I did! I trusted his judgement and his strength. I knew he could overcome. But I had a terrible misgiving about what might happen. Cale was much too quiet. He glanced at me and smiled, and I smiled back. Almost, almost he dispelled my worry. But there was a lingering sadness in his eyes that made my heart drop into my belly.

—

Things got better as we neared the city. I wasn't sure why I felt that way, since the closer we got, the more of Lucas's associates we found. But each nest of evil we found, Cale uprooted entirely, trouncing them with his sword and chasing them off with their figurative tails between their legs.

I supposed even at the time that this was a bad thing. Lucas would no doubt be fully aware of our movements and the exact level of our strength. He would be waiting for us, and he would be hopping mad. I knew him well enough to imagine.

But my spirits lifted in spite of my worry as I saw Cale victorious over increasing numbers of powerful enemies, and had my chance to help as well, in my own inadequate way. Everywhere we went, oblivious people responded with startled amazement at Cale—never knowing the full extent of what he had done for them, but understanding that something momentous had passed. I felt I could almost see the strands of Otherworld weaving together with this one.

By the time we reached the city's centre, we found that news had been circulating about Cale's work, particularly in the country with the tapestry factory. He was being hailed as a hero, a philanthropist, a giant. One newspaper called him "Superman", another suggested he run for political office. One headline even went so far as to say "Mr. Kynsey is exactly what this city needs to save it from the domination of power–hungry tyrants like Lucas Fulbright." Yes, Lucas would be quite angry.

I was surprised when instead of taking me back to the little homely apartment in the suburbs, he drove me straight into the heart of the city and pulled up in front of a tall hotel where a valet parked the car. I craned my neck up at the place, then looked sceptically at Cale.

"Keeping a low profile, are we?" I asked.

He ducked his head with a little smile. "There was a time

for that," he said. He put his warm hand on my back, guiding me gently through the revolving door into the marble-and-gold lobby.

We were expected. The concierge didn't wait for us to come to the desk, but sent a manager immediately to dance attendance on us. It was strange, seeing Cale given the pomp and circumstance due to him in this world.

"Mr. Kynsey," the manager said smoothly, not quite concealing the awe in her eyes. "Allow me to show you to your suite." She snapped her fingers and a bellhop smoothly snatched up the suitcases from our hands.

She took us into the elevator, frowning away a pair of potential passengers until Cale invited them to join us. She glanced at him in surprise, then gave a sheepish smile. She spoke the whole way to the room about restaurants and pools and spas. I clung to Cale's arm, excited about the royal treatment, but still concerned about Lucas's anger.

At last we were alone in our suite, the penthouse, to be exact. After exploring the various rooms, I joined Cale where he brooded on the terrace. His forehead was furrowed in thought, but he relaxed into a smile when I slipped under his arm.

"Penny for your thoughts?" I asked.

"Oh, just thinking about the future." He said, jerking his chin forward. I turned my eyes out to follow his line of sight, and froze.

I would recognize that building anywhere, and the apartment within. It was Lucas's penthouse, a block away, so near that I could see into the great glass walls of his eyrie. It might have been my imagination, but I thought I could see a tall, slim, dark figure watching back at us from the windows. I drew back with a shudder, but Cale held me close, his strong arm comforting.

"Don't worry, my Emma," he said. "It won't be easy, but we will overcome."

"I believe you," I said, burrowing my face into his chest. "I do." I did, really. But I was still afraid of what overcoming would cost.

—

"What's this?" I asked, peering over Cale's shoulder. He was holding an invitation of some sort. I skimmed over the elaborate script. "A banquet? Tonight? In your honour? How fantastic!"

"Hmm," Cale said noncommittally.

"So, when were you going to tell me about this? Are we going?" I asked, draping my arms around his shoulders and giving him a squeeze. "Wouldn't you like to go and rub Lucas's nose in your success? Do you think it would be safe?"

Cale laughed at my barrage of questions. "Lucas Fulbright's mood has very little bearing on my choices, since he will be taken down, no matter how upset I make him. But yes, we will go, and yes, it will be safe enough. When Lucas gets around to trying to kill me, it won't be in a room full of adoring fans." He said that with a grimness that I missed then, engrossed as I was in the intoxicating feeling of his invincibility. It was only later that I remembered the faraway look in his eyes, as though he was witnessing something not yet come to pass in my history.

I gave him another squeeze and spun away from his desk, in search of my purse.

"We'd better get something to wear," I said. "Come on!"

"No need," he said, with a tilt of his head toward the door.

On a bellhop's brass rack, two garment bags hung, one black, one white, both marked with designer labels. I took the white bag and unzipped it, pulling out voluminous lengths of ivory silk chiffon, beaded with tiny crystals and pearls.

"Where did these come from?" I gasped, gently stroking the fine fabric.

"Compliments of the designers, I suppose," Cale said, looking up briefly. "Everyone wants to profit from a rising star."

"You don't seem terribly excited about this," I observed, pulling his chair out and dropping into his lap. I brushed the hair back from his forehead, noticing the creases there.

"I am," he said with a smile. "Don't get me wrong."

"But?" I probed, craning my neck to look up under his down-turned face.

"It doesn't change anything." He said, still not meeting my eyes.

"Okay ..." I was confused. "Fair enough. I get that. People are fickle. I know that more than most. Fame can rise and fall in an instant. Fame isn't everything, anyway. But these people are getting excited about you, and that can't be a bad thing."

"These people have no idea what's coming," he said, with no hint of melodrama in his even voice. "You don't, either."

"Then educate me," I said.

"Don't take this the wrong way," he said, taking my face in his hands and only now looking me in the eye. "But I don't think I could make you understand. Not yet."

"You could try me," I said petulantly. "I'm smarter than you might think."

"It's going to get ugly, Emma. It's going to look like everything's lost. But it won't be. Do you understand? It won't be." His eyes were piercing, and I almost shrank back from the intensity of his stare. But his voice was tender, almost heartbreakingly so, and his hands stroked my hair like a mother would calm a frightened child.

"Forget about that, for now," he said, his face brightening like the sky when the sun breaks through after a storm. "Tonight is a night for celebrating. Tomorrow, we'll go out, just you and me." He ran his thumbs over my brow and kissed me between the eyes.

"Okay, I'd like that." I blinked, bewildered by his behaviour.

"Now, go and relax, get ready for the party." He gave me a playful push off his lap. "I promise I'll be more fun later." I bent to kiss him, then took my dress off to my room.

I hung up the dress on the empty clothes rack in the closet, trying not to compare it to the crimson gown Lucas had given me, the night Cale had rescued me. In fact, I couldn't help but compare the whole experience. Here I was again, getting ready to go out to a ball like Cinderella. But even though it was the same scenario, everything was different.

On that awful night, I had been a prisoner, a captive inside my own body. That pretty dress had been as much a sign of my slavery as a pair of shackles. I had smiled on Lucas's arm, but inside I had been in agony. I had been lost, with no past and no future, longing for a hope I didn't know existed.

But Cale had changed all that. Tonight I would step out of the limo on my own terms, on the arm of a man I loved, and who loved me. And I felt qualified to make that assessment, now that Cale had taught me what love meant. I would show my own face to the world, not some wooden puppet mask. There would be no hiding in shame, no cowering in fear.

I ran a hot bath and slipped in, this time not hoping the water would change me, but revelling in the joy of being changed already. On a whim, I reached over the side of the tub for my mirror in my pants pocket and looked into it. I smiled at the faint reflection in the fogged metal—the three images of me barely flickered at all. I was, and was becoming, myself again.

This time I didn't rely on a maid to paint away the ugliness I felt inside. I let my shoulder–length, strawberry blonde hair go wavy, curling bits here and there. I dusted my face with the barest hint of makeup, letting the beauty Cale had put in me show through in rosy luminescence.

By the time I slid the one–shouldered sheath on and looked in the full–length mirror, I thought no one who had seen me at that other party with Lucas would recognize me as the same girl. But I recognized myself more than ever. The only thing my reflection lacked now was the crown that would mean I was restored to Otherworld at last.

I glanced at the clock—it was time. I put on the finishing touches: a pair of crystal–studded high–heeled sandals and an ethereal necklace of diamonds and pearls all scattered together on tangled threads. Then I crept out of my room in search of Cale.

He was waiting for me, standing tall and handsome near the door. He was in a sleek black suit, complete with black tie, and his hair gelled in perfect disarray.

"I bet it took you five minutes to do that," I said with

mock envy.

He dropped his jaw in wounded pride. "It took all of six," he said, then grinned, holding out his elbow to me. I wrapped my hand around his arm, resting my cheek on him.

"Thank you," I said.

"For what?"

"For rescuing me."

"You already thanked me for that," he said with a smile, stroking my cheek with his free hand.

"Not lately."

—

The sense of incomplete deja–vu didn't end with the preparations. Stepping out of the limo felt like the twilight zone. It took all of my power to remember, in the face of the staccato camera flashes and buzz of talk, to whose arm I clung. But Cale looked down at me, and I smiled gratefully back.

Galvanized, I walked up the red carpet with him, smiling as he answered reporters' questions and answering one or two of my own. I was proud, genuinely proud of him. The most amazing thing was that he was just as proud of me. He could have let me stand in the background, but he brought me forward, much to my chagrin, and introduced me. He told them that I was his partner in everything he had done, and that he wouldn't have chosen another person to share his life with.

"Does that mean we'll be hearing wedding bells in the future?" a female reporter asked, pouting slightly.

"Inevitably," he said, and gathered me close to kiss me. I could see the camera flashes, even with my eyes closed.

I was giddy with excitement and nerves by the time we made it into the hall. The place was gorgeous, all white with tables and candles and people. Out of my new-trained reflex, I pulled my mirror out of my purse to look around for what hidden thugs might be lurking. But Cale pushed my hand down, indicating that I didn't need to look.

"Are we safe?" I murmured.

"Safe enough," he said, with his eyes fixed across the room. I followed his line of sight, and my blood chilled in my veins.

On the other side of the banquet hall, in a well-cut tuxedo, stood Lucas Fulbright. He was speaking with someone, but something in the line of his posture suggested he was just as attuned to our presence as we were to his. He looked toward us, reacted as if mildly surprised, and inclined his head politely before going back to his conversation.

"That was weird," I mused, as Cale pulled out my chair for me.

He didn't comment, still standing.

"I'll get you a drink," he said.

"Are you sure I'll ..."

"You'll be fine," he said.

I watched him go, determined not to show weakness by stealing a glance at Lucas. But I was so conscious of him, standing in the same room as me, that I imagined his eyes burning into my back. It was strange, this mixture of utter loathing and a faint echo of the lust that had lost everything for Cale and me, so long ago. I fixed my eyes on Cale, leaning with debonair grace against the bar, now caught in conversation with some VIP, and tried to forget that anyone else existed.

"A bold move, coming here," a voice said behind me, a voice that froze my blood.

"Pardon me?" I said, whirling to see Lucas standing over me. My hand went to my Otherworld sword that only three people in the room could see.

"Ah, I see, pleading ignorance for the benefit of the audience. Allow me to introduce myself—Lucas Fulbright." He extended his hand. I shrank back. "Come, come. Surely you can muster a show of manners."

"Emma Delaney," I said, putting my hand in his as though into the mouth of a crocodile. To my great horror, he kissed my hand with courtly manners. When he released me, I resisted the urge to make a show of wiping it off, though I did rub the back of my hand surreptitiously on the skirt of my dress.

"As I was saying, it is surprising to see Mr. Kynsey here in the city. I would have thought he'd prefer to keep you in the country." There was a definite challenge in his words.

"You'll find I'm not the same girl you had under your thumb," I said, the steel in my voice emphasized by the sword across my lap.

Lucas leaned close, trapping me against the back of my chair. He spoke softly, but his words couldn't have been more effective if he'd shouted them. "Oh, yes, my Emma, you are exactly the same girl you've always been. You still haven't resolved that attraction you had for me from the very beginning. You still wouldn't last long with Cale ordering you around, no matter how infatuated you might be right now. And you know, in your deepest fears, that the minute Cale let you out of his sight, you'd be right back where you started—drugged on Ambrosia and languishing in my bed."

"You're wrong," I said flatly, mortified by the trembling in my voice.

"I see you've met *my* Emma," Cale said pleasantly over my shoulder, brooking no mistakes about his claim on me with the emphasis on the possessive. Lucas retreated from me at once, and I breathed a sigh of relief.

"I see you've stooped to common kidnapping and brute violence," Lucas nearly purred as he recovered his nerves. He eyed Cale up and down. "Making a show are we? I trust you haven't forgotten where things stand between us?"

"Not for a second," Cale said, his voice quiet but sharp-edged. "But your time hasn't come yet." He gave Lucas a hard stare, and the latter visibly shrank back before he turned away and fled smoothly out of the room.

"What was all that about?" I asked Cale, my heart still pounding.

"Nothing you need concern yourself with at the moment," he replied, prying my sword from my clenched fingers. He sheathed it for me, and put the slim stem of a wine glass into my hand. "Drink this, you'll feel a bit calmer."

I sipped at the wine, and I did feel better. But as I smiled through the dinner and the dancing and the guests and the paparazzi, I felt a lingering unease saturate me. It wasn't worry for Cale. I had seen enough to know that he would hold his own in any fight, and even Lucas was no match for him. In fact, I had never been so confident of Cale's assured victory.

No, the problem wasn't Cale. It was me.

—

It was quite late when I stumbled out of bed in the morning, and even later when I came out of my room, showered and dressed, for breakfast. I remembered shedding the designer gown and falling into bed the night before, but only vaguely.

Cale, by contrast, looked like he'd already been up for hours. He was reading by the window, in a beam of sunlight that lit up his white shirt like he was glowing. I grabbed a bagel from the breakfast tray and went over to sit with him, picking up a newspaper that caught my interest.

I realized right away what had attracted my eye. It was Cale's name, Cale's face on the front page. It was our picture, in fact, starry eyed and smiling on the red carpet last night. But the headline surprised me.

"*Cale Kynsey: What is he after?*" I read the bold print aloud. Incredulous, I skimmed further, picking out the pertinent lines. "Ulterior motives? You?" I asked. "*... just another mob boss...dark secrets...continued on page 3: 'Kynsey escort scandal'...*" I turned the page, rattling the noisy paper in my haste.

My heart fell as I saw my picture—last night, smiling and beautiful in my white dress, side by side with an image from the fateful gala where I stood as a puppet prisoner beside Lucas, dark and mysterious with my black hair and burgundy ball gown. Further down the page, I saw a rather fuzzy but unmistakeable photo of me, in my short skirt and stilettos, leaning invitingly into a car window.

I let out a cry of dismay as I read the article, an unfortunately true bit of smutty gossip. Now the whole world knew that Cale Kynsey, that perfect paragon of a Prince, was with a two-bit prostitute. Now, by association, he was cast as black as Lucas. As black as I. I closed my eyes in defeat and shame, closing the newspaper and putting it aside.

"I'm so, so sorry," I said, turning my head away from Cale and burying my face in my hands.

Then Cale's arms were around me, his voice gentle in my ear. "I thought I said you weren't allowed to say that anymore."

"It makes me so very angry, what they say about you," I said, clinging to him tearfully.

"Don't let it get to you. It's just Lucas. It's all he can do, you know—talk. He doesn't have any real clout."

"But the people who wrote this—the people who threw that party for you—how can they show one face to you and another to him?"

"Lucas promises them what they want," he said with a shrug. "It satisfies in the short run. But I appeal to them because they know I have what they need. They long for Otherworld, but they don't know it."

"Then let's bring it to them!" I said fiercely.

"We will, my warrior Princess. Tomorrow." He smiled at my fervour. "But first, today and tonight belong to us, just you and me. We'll shut the world out for a little while."

—

We spent the day on the water, enjoying the last gasp of the summer's sun. It was quite warm and pleasant, and a good day to have a picnic. As the afternoon wore on, we returned to the hotel to change for dinner, then Cale took me to a quaint little Italian restaurant. The maitre d' led us to a quiet back room with no questions. He knew Cale's face, but he knew equally well how to keep his counsel.

The meal was fantastic, perhaps the best I'd ever had. But that could have been just as much because of the company. I leaned close to Cale, breathing him in. He seemed to be doing the same—almost as though he were storing me up against a long famine. It was disconcerting, but I couldn't allow it to spoil this perfect moment.

I was excited. It seemed like at long last, things were lining up to bring Otherworld back. I couldn't wait to see my home again, to see things made right again. More than that, I couldn't wait to see Lucas brought low and powerless. I didn't like the thought that he was out there, lurking, able to destroy all the tenuous peace that Cale had built for us. As long as Lucas was free to oppose us, I was still not completely free. And my full emancipation would begin tomorrow.

After dinner, when we were enjoying dessert, Cale pulled apart from me a little so he could look into my eyes. He was serious, his grey–green eyes intense with love and deep with feeling. My heart quickened at the look he was giving me. I knew it meant something very important.

"Do you remember the first day—that first day when I made you?" he asked.

"Yes," I whispered, and my mind conjured up my new-found memory of a sun–drenched clearing filled with moss and trees and flowers, and a shining prince.

"I asked you to marry me one day."

"I remember," I said, touching the place where his ring used to rest, and I felt my betrayal anew like a fresh wound. "But I lost the ring."

"That doesn't matter," he said. "We can start again." He pulled a small box out from his pocket and opened it for me. Inside was a gorgeous ring of white gold chased in the knot-work emblem of Otherworld, set with diamonds. It was like nothing you'd ever see in a modern jeweller's store. Either he'd had it made specially, or it came from Otherworld. Judging by the unearthly glow that kindled faintly in the depths of the stones, I guessed the latter.

I gasped as he put the ring on my finger.

"I promise you, my Emma," he said, his eyes still holding mine, "That I will take you as my wife, when the time is right. You are my Princess, from this day on. No matter where I may go, I will come again without fail, to take you with me one day and make a home with you forever."

I was bereft of speech at that moment, and it seemed enough for him when I leaned into his kiss and embraced him. When we broke apart, I looked at him, my eyes shining with love.

"I promise, too," I said. "I will never fall away again."

He put his finger on my lips. "Don't promise things beyond your control," he said. "It will only bring you pain."

His words stung me more than I thought possible. "Why do you doubt me? After all we've been through? I would go to death and back with you!" I wanted to believe those words, myself, even more than I wanted him to believe them. I felt that perhaps if I could convince him, that would be enough. But I couldn't help but think about Lucas's taunting, his accusations.

"Emma, my Emma," he said soothingly. "You'll regret saying these things. But know this—no matter what you say or do, I still love you."

"I have to use the restroom," I said stiffly, and slithered out of my seat. I didn't look at him, because I wanted to stay mad. The restroom was empty, thank goodness, and I leaned on the counter, staring at my fuming self in the mirror.

It irked me, the things Cale was saying. After all the words he'd spoken, building up my confidence in myself, saying it didn't matter, telling me my betrayal was in the past—now he called my loyalty into question? After everything he had done for me, did he really think I was that fickle?

What I really didn't want to admit was that I feared he was right. I hadn't liked my reaction to Lucas—that any part of me might welcome seeing him again. I didn't like that the nearer to the city we got, the more tense or exciting the situation, the more I craved the old release of Ambrosia. How sick was I, to long for slavery again?

No, I didn't want to admit that even a part of me had entertained that thought, so it was easier for me to concede the point to Cale and pretend that his words, and mine, hadn't been said. I would rewind our evening to the perfect part, just after Cale had proposed to me and I had accepted, and we would go on in blissful love. I fixed my lipstick, and left the restroom in search of my fiancé.

—

As I had hoped, Cale was willing to overlook our little lovers' quarrel and the evening continued sweetly. We drove around the city, and lost in conversation with my beloved, I wasn't paying attention to where we were going, until we pulled up to the curb and Cale turned off the car.

"Where are we?" I asked, intrigued.

"Don't you recognize it?"

I looked out my window, frowning at the darkened greenspace beyond the curb. Then the moon came out from behind a cloud, and I remembered.

There was a silver–blue lawn, and a bench overlooking a city view, with the dark lace of the trees framing the full moon. I looked at the scene with mingled enthusiasm and apprehension. This was the place we'd gone, the night I'd truly fallen in love with Cale—again. I remembered cool grass on my bare feet, and falling asleep on his shoulder, after listening to him tell me all about how I'd loved him once before.

But I couldn't forget where we were, only blocks away from the corner where I had once paced under a street light, where Cale had first appeared to save me, where Lucas waited in his seedy warehouse like a king in his throne room. I wanted to use my mirror to look around, but I relied on Cale, instead.

"Are we safe, here?" I asked.

"Perfectly, for tonight," he said. He got out of the car and came around to open my door. On a whim, I took off my shoes like I had that first time. Then, hand in hand, we set off for the bench together, like some kind of Adam and Eve in Eden. The hum of traffic, the lights below, none of that mattered right now. Tonight we were alone, together.

For a long while, we sat and talked about everything. Then Cale said he just wanted to think, but if I could just be with him, he'd be happy. I watched the sky for a while, then my head became heavy and I laid it on his shoulder. Before I knew it, I was sleeping. I only realized I had fallen asleep when my neck bobbed and Cale gently laid my head in his lap.

"I'm sorry," I said. "I must have dozed off."

"I missed you," he said with a smile that looked sad. It might have been my imagination, I told myself. He stroked my hair, looking at me. I tried to keep my eyes open, to hold his steady gaze as long as I could, but sleep got the better of me one more time.

I was conscious of waking many times through that night, aware of the passage of long hours. I had impressions of Cale's face in torment, but I couldn't tell if I dreamed it or not. At last, I opened my eyes and dawn was breaking across the sky. I sat up with a groan, stretching, and looked at Cale. It wasn't my imagination, or a dream. He definitely seemed sad. This wasn't the face of a Prince before an assured victory, with his beloved firmly by his side. This was the look of a man in the face of a momentous sacrifice, and I didn't understand it.

"What is it, love?" I asked, reaching out to touch him.

"Our night is over," he said, wistfully. "Now the real work starts."

I examined his face, trying to make sense of the deep sorrow that had washed away all the ebullient confidence and lavish adoration of the past few months. I had a sinking feeling that I had missed something significant in the night, some silent turning point. I instantly regretted sleeping through a single moment of our night together.

I put my feet down on the dew–damp grass, and as I did, I was aware of a strange sensation of difference in the space behind me. I knew at once we weren't alone. I turned, confirming my worst fears. There was a burly man standing behind our bench—one I recognized as Lucas's man. I pulled out my mirror and saw him as he truly was, a hundred times more fearsome and horrible than he appeared in this shadow world. But worse than that, I saw in the mirror that he hadn't come alone.

I stood, drawing my sword and holding it at the ready against this band of dark warriors. They were numerous, but I knew Cale could take them, with little to no help from me. He stood beside me, but something was wrong. He moved too slowly. His stance was too lax. I cast a glance at him and saw him standing tall, his hands empty and open.

"What are you doing?" I asked in shock. "Aren't you going to fight?"

He didn't answer, but he unstrapped his sword from his waist and surrendered it, scabbard and all, to the only visible thug. The man smirked evilly, taking the sword and giving a quiet order. I didn't have to use my mirror to know that the invisible hordes were advancing on us. With a frustrated cry, I turned away from Cale's incomprehensible behaviour and swung out blindly with my blade. It was useless. I felt unseen hands clamp down on my arms, my legs, my hair. My sword was wrenched from my hands.

"It's going to be alright, my Emma," Cale said softly, turning a tormented yet serene face toward me.

"How?" I shouted. "How is it going to be alright, Cale? Tell me that?"

The invisible hands brought me to the man I could see, and he took my arm in his iron grip. I tried to wrench free, but he only laughed.

"Just let him take us," Cale said, and the words rocked through me.

9

He was giving up. After all we'd done, after all he'd promised, now, when it got down to the real thing, he was giving up!

I was furious. But a small, rational part of my mind told me there was no point in struggling. I couldn't make a dent in a single one of Lucas's army if I didn't have Cale fighting for me. With a sullen, confused glance at my beloved—who seemed more like a stranger to me now than the first night he'd come to save me—I stopped struggling and let the thug lead me away.

They took us to a sleek black car with tinted windows and nudged me inside. Cale followed, pushed with more force than was necessary. I didn't speak to him, still angry, but the misery in his face struck me, and I offered my hand under cover of our legs as the car pulled out into the road and squealed into a U–turn. I noticed that someone else was bringing Cale's car. They would be careful to leave no trace of us.

I worried Cale's fingers nervously between my own until he gave me a squeeze I guessed was meant to be reassuring. It was hard to know what to think. I knew how Lucas worked, especially now with my memory restored. But that didn't give me any measure of confidence. It only reminded me of how devious, how manipulative, how violent, how utterly evil he was. It was all I could do to keep myself from trembling in fear.

I might have been okay, going into this, if I knew what to expect from Cale. A day ago, I would have been certain that Cale would come out swinging, felling the enemy left and right, and pinning Lucas into a corner until he cowered. But this Cale, so quiet and grave beside me, I didn't know. I had no way of predicting how he would react. I waited for the moment he would throw this all aside—some pretence to get through Lucas's defences. But it just didn't seem like the bold and fearless Cale I knew.

The car stopped, under the looming shadow of the warehouse. My heart kicked into high gear, hammering away as I got out of the car as calmly and fluidly as I could manage. I was determined that no matter what happened, I wouldn't give Lucas the satisfaction of seeing how afraid I really was.

The warehouse was dark, except for one light hanging over Lucas's desk. He sat there, watching us come in as he leaned back casually in his chair. He was smiling, just a little, and dressed impeccably in a suit. When our captors marched us up to the desk, Lucas looked back and forth between us, still smiling. But there was a gleam of malignant triumph in his eyes that I didn't miss, and something more as well—fear.

I had to admit, Lucas knew how to put on a show. He stood up from the desk and walked around behind us. As he passed me, I felt my skin crawl, but I didn't move. Still, after all of this, he didn't speak. He returned to the desk, as though satisfied that we were who we appeared to be, and folded his arms.

"Well, well, well, Prince Kaehl," Lucas sneered. "It's a sorry thing to see our business come to this. Stooping to kidnapping, murder and theft. I didn't think you could."

"I'm just reclaiming what's mine," Cale said evenly.

"Yours? Well, now, do you mean the land that is mine by conquest, after you so cruelly threw me out of your shining Kingdom? I know you've long desired to steal it back to Otherworld. Well, you'll find I've made it hard to do that. This piece of real estate is so twisted up, it wouldn't look too pretty next to your perfect world.

"Or perhaps you mean this lovely little creature?" He circled the desk again and came to stand beside me, stroking my hair. He glimpsed my hand and snatched it before I could act.

"Oh! Does this mean you two are engaged? Am I the first to hear the glad news?" His voice dripped with scorn. He pulled the ring from my finger viciously and held it up for Cale to see.

"Did you think you could whisk her out from under my eyes? All due respect, your Highness, but you can't take someone else's property without asking." With a sudden twist of his wrist, he gripped my jaw and turned my face to look up at him. I glared back with defiant eyes.

"Oh, I can see why you might want to come back for the princess you once loved," Lucas continued, looking appraisingly into my eyes. Then he twisted my face in the other direction, forcing me to look at Cale. He gazed back steadily, and I flinched away from the pain etched in his eyes. "But you have to admit, she's not the same girl you made. I take that as a point of pride, you know. You made her to your specifications. Now I've remade her to mine.

"You know, I don't understand it. What do you see in her, that you would risk everything to come here? You could just make another Princess for your perfect Kingdom. Why go to all the trouble to get this one back, with all her obvious flaws?"

"I love her," Cale said simply, still staring into my eyes.

"Awwww, hear that, princess?" Lucas derisively shoved my face away and let go. "He loves you. So much, in fact, that he got you all excited about fixing all the ills of the world, all for nothing. He knows that you can't go back. You can never go back to Otherworld tainted as you are. You are a creature of my domain now, forever. So you see, he built you up with lofty dreams and false hopes, and then dumped you right into my lap. That's what he's done, you realize? There will be no getting out of this—for you, or for him."

Lucas turned his attention back to Cale, and so did I. I had the sickening feeling that for once, Lucas was telling the truth. "Or did you think you could pull one over on me, playing meek? Waltzing right into my lair and taking me by surprise? Don't suffer any illusions, noble prince. She is mine. I will do what I want with her."

Lucas had his hands around my neck in a moment, and squeezed viciously. My eyes bulged in surprise, and I clawed reflexively at his grip. I tried to scream, but the sound came out as a strangled gurgle.

"I've kept her all these years. But now and then, I tire of her. You understand?" he smirked at Cale. "No, of course you don't. But nevertheless, I will do with her—or dispose of her—as I will."

"I'm prepared to pay for her," Cale said, his voice full of urgency.

Lucas's hands relaxed, only slightly, and the red haze that had started to creep across my vision receded.

"Whatever it takes," Cale added. His grim face, the lips

pressed tight together, the crease of anguish between the eyes, was all the proof anyone needed of his sincerity.

"You know there's only one price I'll accept."

I didn't like the sound of that.

"Done," Cale said. The hands opened and I collapsed forward onto my knees, gasping in the fetid air of the old warehouse.

What had Cale just given away? He couldn't possibly have given his Kingdom for me. No, he loved Otherworld too much. He couldn't see his beautiful world destroyed by this tyrant. But what else could it be? Why was Cale so silent?

"This is going to end here. It's going to end badly for you. Did you think I'd be happy with my miserable little corner of the world? I won't be satisfied until everything is under my dominion. Otherworld will be mine, and I will take great pleasure in turning it to my will, just as I have done with your pure little maiden." He laughed at his joke, and the muscles in my jaw tightened against the shame and rage that overwhelmed me. I couldn't look at Cale, couldn't bear to face the truth in his eyes. I was as Lucas implied—weak and defiled. I didn't have to look in my magic mirror to know that. What Cale had offered me was a fairy tale. It wasn't real.

"You could have cut your losses and gone back," Lucas said, pacing behind his desk. "You can, even now, but somehow, I doubt you will." He pinned Cale with an intense glare, leaning over the desk towards his opponent, his eyes probing for any sign of caving. I saw the wicked gleam of triumph as he knew he had won, and Otherworld was his for the taking. Cale still made no move. When—when would he show his power? Why was he so silent?

"Just as I thought," Lucas confirmed. He turned his back. At some unseen command, his enforcers advanced.

The only thing that kept me from screaming just then was my sheer will to survive. In hindsight that was just an excuse. It was cowardice, plain and simple, that held my tongue. Lucas whirled back to face us, and suddenly the bottom dropped out of my world.

We were in Otherworld—I knew it at once. But the transition was so abrupt that I stumbled and fell to my knees, as though the ground had suddenly tilted. Though the sky was grey, it was still brighter than Lucas's warehouse, and I squinted to see. There was the dusty plain with its ugly, squat ziggurat, flying Leyukas's banner in defiant mockery. I looked behind me and saw the dark wood of Iffreyn closing in around the shadowed path I had walked so long ago. This was the clearing where I had looked my last on Otherworld, so long ago. This was the place I had first tasted Ambrosia.

The thought of the drug overpowered me, and I began to tremble. If I had just one shot—one taste, I could forget about this whole sorry mess. I could forget about Cale and how he had wooed me with an impossible fairy tale. I clenched my fists and fought the rising nausea in my stomach.

Lucas's army formed a ring around the three of us. They called and jeered in a deafening roar. But I had ears only for Lucas's soft taunts … and for Cale, if only he would speak.

Lucas, or rather, Leyukas, for now he was his Otherworldly self, circled Cale like a vulture. Cale—the Prince Kaehl as I had once known him, regal in his robes and starred crown. I could feel the arid wind stirring my long hair, and knew I was changed too. But my crown was gone, and my once pure white gown was torn and stained with drugged drink, as it had been when I had parted from Kaehl.

Leyukas took out a wicked-looking dagger, wielding it with purpose over Kaehl's statuesque body. I saw the moment of action and I gasped in spite of myself.

But Leyukas did not stab. He slashed at the pure white robes, and they fell around Kaehl's feet in shreds, revealing the beautiful male form that he had saved for me. I had so wanted to see this. But not now, not like this. I turned my head in shame.

"Do you see?" Leyukas shouted for the benefit of his minions. "He bleeds!"

I looked back to see a thin line of blood on Kaehl's chest that slowly spread and wept across his skin. Leyukas dragged his dagger parallel to the first cut, and again. Kaehl's face pinched with pain, but he kept from crying out.

"Come and see for yourselves!" Leyukas called, and his army came with a roar. I struggled to my feet, hunching in on myself as they pressed against me from all sides in their eagerness to avenge themselves on Kaehl. I hardly felt their jostling, but strained for a glimpse of my lover through the hordes.

I could only see flashes, but the images I saw were seared on my mind like sudden lightning, intensified by adrenaline, terror, and grief—his lean limbs twisting in the grasp of his enemies, blood blooming from a fresh cut on his thigh, purple-red-black contusions that swelled so that his human form was less and less recognizable, his face, contorted in agony, disfigured and speckled with the ricochet of his own blood.

I wanted to tell Lucas to stop, to leave him alone. But I didn't know what I could do, with Cale so apathetic. Did he expect me to speak out? What did he think I could do, without his help? I grappled with the urge to save him from this, and the sure knowledge that there was nothing I could do but die with him. I chewed on my lip until I tasted my own blood.

At last, the seething sea of brutality ebbed, and I almost fell again without the buttressing effect of the press of bodies. I stumbled, willing myself to stand upright and face Leyukas defiantly.

He was lost in contemplation of his cruel masterpiece, with a wistful, joyous look that made me want to vomit. He circled Kaehl, who was still miraculously standing. Only then did he seem to remember my presence.

"Well, well, my Immah," he purred. "My little princess whore. What do you think of your precious prince now?"

I flinched away, but couldn't really keep myself from looking at Kaehl. He looked back, his eyes all but obscured by swollen flesh and dripping blood. But I could still see the love in their grey–green depths, and it struck me to the core. *Is this how you love me?* I thought. By leaving me to his mercy when you surely could have beaten him to a pulp? But I kept those words to myself. I wouldn't give Leyukas the satisfaction of seeing me fold.

But in the midst of what I thought was strength, I lived my weakest moment, and in fighting Lucas's control, I gave in more completely than I could have thought possible.

"Tell me, my Immah," Leyukas came close to my ear. "Does he mean anything to you? Can you follow a man like that? Love a man like that?"

He made a little flourish of his hand, and something materialized on a nearby flat–topped boulder. It was a small ordinary object, but I knew at once what it was, or more importantly what it held. Cradled within the plain darkened pewter cup was a pool of glimmering crimson liquid, like the juice of rubies. I felt a fine tremor run through me, and my eyes flicked back and forth from the cup of Ambrosia to Kaehl.

I saw the blood flowing in runnels, mingled with sweat, over Kaehl's once-perfect, now-broken skin. I saw the knife in Leyukas's hand, and the look of assured triumph in his eyes. There was nothing like that in Kaehl's demeanor right now. There was only pain and defeat. No matter how much he may love me, I was lost. There was no future for me, without him. To my utter shock, he lowered and raised his shattered jaw almost imperceptibly, but I knew from the force of his gaze that he had nodded to me. Something snapped inside me at that moment.

"I don't know what to think," I said, quite honestly.

"I'll tell you what you think," Leyukas said, turning my face to look into his eyes. He looked hungry for the win. "You think you made a mistake."

I made no response.

"Say it!" he roared. I flinched.

"I made a mistake," I repeated in a small voice.

"You are my Immah."

"I am y—your Immah."

"You never loved him."

"I...I never loved him," I said.

"Say it again!" Leyukas commanded, turning me back to Kaehl. "Say it to him."

I couldn't meet Kaehl's eyes, but I didn't miss the steady look he gave me, and the depth of love that he had for me, even now.

"I never loved you," I whispered.

"Now, kiss me," Leyukas said, and helped me to it. Savagely. I wanted to cry more than ever, then, but I was past the ability to weep. He released me with an evil, dreamy smile and walked over to Kaehl.

"I doubt she ever kissed you like that," he taunted, then smashed Kaehl heavily across the face with the back of his hand.

The drug was calling to me, so close on its rock pedestal. Ambrosia was my only friend right now, the only thing that could blot out my pain and erase all memory of Kaehl. It would be better to forget he existed, to walk around half–dead, than to live with this feeling of loss and guilt. But I knew better than to ask right now.

Leyukas wasn't done yet. He held up my ring, letting the dull sun glint through it.

"Oh, and this belongs to you," he said. "I'm not a thief—I wouldn't take something that isn't mine." He put the ring into Kaehl's hand and closed his fingers into a fist around it. Then, with a malicious glare, he tightened his hand until several of Kaehl's fingers cracked audibly.

I drew in my breath sharply and silently at the agony in Kaehl's face. But it wasn't over. They continued on—the monsters of Leyukas's army—administering their atrocities until there wasn't an inch of flesh or bone on Kaehl that hadn't been bloodied, bruised or broken. They were doing a most thorough job, and enjoying every minute.

Then the clearing came to an abrupt hush, at some unseen command. Leyukas stepped up to Kaehl, who was now on his knees. He lifted up his beaten adversary by the hair, smiling a little crooked grin.

"You've lost," he crooned in Kaehl's ear. "You've lost everything, because you couldn't admit that I was better than you. Well, now everyone knows."

"I haven't lost everything," Kaehl gasped through gritted teeth.

"No? Oh, you mean *her*?" Leyukas looked at me and the peels of his harsh laughter echoed back from the mountainsides. Rage spiralled up my throat and choked me. "That's the most delicious irony of all! You gave up your life, and—let's face it—your kingdom as well to save this pitiful excuse for a princess. But did it ever occur to you that in her heart of hearts she doesn't want to be saved? Look at her! Even now, she wants it. My Ambrosia."

He was right. My eyes had wandered again to the dully gleaming cup. Caught, I burned with shame and looked down at my feet. I wanted to strangle Leyukas for adding to Kaehl's torture with these words, but I couldn't deny the truth of them. I did want the Ambrosia. The call of oblivion was growing louder by the second, like a physical hunger.

"You saved her, you set her free at the cost of everything else, but she'll willingly walk back into my arms the moment you are gone. So really, you've gained nothing."

Leyukas let go of Kaehl's hair and he slumped back to the ground, exhausted. Then Leyukas took the star–set crown from Kaehl's head, raised it over his own, and …

I blinked. Leyukas's mob let out a collective outcry. Kaehl looked up at his enemy with a steel–edged glare beneath his bloody brows. Leyukas stood there, shocked out of his arrogance, with empty hands. The crown of Otherworld was gone.

The air around me shuddered, and suddenly the illusion was broken. I fell to my knees again, and this time I did vomit. I raised my eyes and looked directly into Cale's face, bruised and swollen and dead-eyed, with a trickling bullet hole in the centre of his forehead. With a cry, I scrambled back, looking up at Lucas, bewildered. He stood over me, the proverbial smoking gun in his hand.

This was all Lucas's lackeys would have seen—their impeccably dressed mob boss taking out a rival with the simple, quiet efficiency of a silenced gun.

"Get him out of here," Lucas said, laying the gun aside. "Sloane, clean her up and take care of her. And Emma … cheer up. Soon enough it will be back to the way it was."

I watched two burly men pick up Cale's limp body and carry it away to some ignominious end at the bottom of the river. What a dishonourable end for such a magnificent prince. I wanted to run after them, to throw myself on his lifeless body and tell them they could only take it if they killed me too. But there was no use. Cale was dead, and I had thrown in my lot with Lucas … again.

Oh, how I hated myself then. I hardly felt Sloane lift me to my feet or lead me to my room. My eyes were too blurred to see anything. He helped me to a chair and leaned close with a heavy sigh.

"I'm so sorry princess." He rested a heavy hand on my shoulder.

I flinched away from the touch and twitched my outstretched arm.

"Just get it over with."

Just let me forget.

His eyes were on me with concern, but I didn't meet his gaze. I looked at the wall as the needle went in, delivering me from myself.

Back to the way it was, Lucas had said. I would soon forget Cale, and Otherworld, and even how horrible Lucas really was. But the difference was that this time, when I dreamed of a prince coming to rescue me, no one would come.

—

After months of real dreams, a night's sleep under the influence of Ambrosia was a bit of a shock, to say the least. I don't know whether I actually screamed or only imagined I did. But I certainly kept the other girls awake. I couldn't even say what scared me so much.

There were disjointed images that later I could only almost recall, as though the Ambrosia had set up some kind of curtain in my mind that shrouded the memories but couldn't completely obscure them.

I saw a strange place that I felt I should remember—a beautiful and lush valley. But as I watched the lushness withered and the valley was flat and devoid of beauty. I saw a noble prince, perfect in every way you'd expect him to be. I loved him, in my drugged dream. I felt a malevolent presence, and suddenly the beautiful prince was ruined, his mutilated body held aloft on a pole for a cheering army to view. A dark–hooded warlord stood on the top of a stepped pyramid, a black banner unfurling in the hot wind overhead. I knew that man, and I feared him.

The man took me by the arms and kissed me, then with a smile, I held out my wrists for a pair of iron shackles.

—

"Princess?" a voice woke me in the evening, and I started. I rolled over and stared at the figure in the door, uncomprehending. It seemed right that I should be called by that name, but not here, not now.

"It's me, princess. Sloane."

I recognized him now, but in the fuzzy way that Ambrosia allowed.

"I'm sorry," he said. "I'm sorry how things turned out. I didn't have anything to do with it, you know."

"'S okay," I said, though I was a little hazy on what he was apologizing for. I knew a great sadness and fear that had roused me through the night with screams and sweats, and that was all.

"Time to get dressed. Lucas tells me you'll be working tonight, though I didn't think it was best."

I shrugged and got out of bed, putting on a few bits of clothes and some makeup to hide the effects of tears I couldn't recall shedding. My hair colour didn't seem quite right, other things out of place. Sloane kept watching me carefully, but I wasn't made of glass, I wasn't going to break.

He walked me out to my corner. I paced for a little while, unsure of what I should be doing. My eyes kept wandering to a streetlamp across the road, a pool of light that I felt shouldn't be empty. I had a vague vision of a figure under that light. A figure walking across the street towards me.

A car drove up, and a man rolled down the window and leaned out, inviting. I looked up at Sloane, who urged me to get in. I leaned forward with a smile, then a slight frown as the face didn't match what I expected. The man frowned back, then pulled back into the car and pealed away from my corner. I stood upright, dismayed.

"Princess, you've got to try harder," Sloane said from the shadows. "Take care. I don't want to see you hurt. Play nice for the next one."

Before long, another car rolled up. Someone who knew me, but again didn't fit the unconscious criteria I was judging by. With a quick glance at Sloane, who was motioning encouragingly to me, I stepped up to the car and leaned down, smiling. The car door opened, and I stepped in.

"Hi, Baby," said the man, who clearly knew me well. His hand rested possessively on my leg.

I recovered from my blank confusion quickly, and smiled. "Hi, yourself. Did you miss me?"

He drove away, and I looked out the window at Sloane. It was all coming back to me, far too easily.

—

Lucas came to reward me personally that morning. He seemed to intimate that I ought to feel pleased by his attentions. But I didn't feel anything. He also seemed to be watching me, carefully, for a sign of something. He seemed inordinately nervous for a man who held all the cards. He was very interested in a pocket mirror of mine that he found face–down on the dresser. He asked if he could keep it, but I didn't care.

That day I had a rough sleep again, haunted with images that might have been memories or dreams—I didn't know. I woke plagued with guilt for something I didn't even know I'd done, again wet with tears shed for some unknown loss. I prepared for the night, making something beautiful out of a face and body that I would always think of as ugly. And I went out into the dark looking for some unknown thing that I feared, with a pang of sad certainty, would never come.

—

Dawn came again after that second night, though for some reason I couldn't think why it should. Another day seemed pointless. Sloane took me up to my room, my reward in hand.

I waited at the table, as I thought must be usual. I felt so weary, so lost—I put my head down on the table, and tears began to flow.

"What's wrong, princess?" Sloane soothed, putting down the syringe and patting my hair paternally.

"Wish I knew," I sighed.

"I know it's hard ever since he...well, ever since you came back. But you'll be right as rain, soon. You'll see." Sloane seemed to be trying to cheer himself up, just as much as me. "It's important that you try hard, pet. You've just got to make it a little longer and everything will be okay. Keep Lucas happy, and he'll do well by you."

"I guess," I moped. The blood was starting to sing in my ears, calling its siren song for the drug, and I stretched out my arm impatiently.

"Sorry, princess," he said with a little laugh. "Here's your bit, and welcome to it. You've been through enough to deserve a little rest." He deftly delivered my dose, and closed up the packet.

The dreams were on me before I even hit the bed. I was vaguely aware of Sloane helping me under the covers, but I fought him—fought the grasping and jostling bodies that crowded against me, hiding something from my sight. It was something important, I knew.

At once, the crowd parted, and I stood on a dry, arid plain. We all gazed up at the same thing—a singular moment that I somehow felt would define the universe forever. Two figures grappled at the top of a black obsidian ziggurat, under a black and crimson flag. One dark, one gleaming with perfect light. I held my breath, waiting for that all-important outcome. The figures overbalanced, toppled from the heights. The flag tore in the violent wind and fluttered away.

I woke gasping for air, and the dream fled.

—

The wash of streetlights was soothing as I tooled around the city in car after car. Bright and dark. Bright and dark. I gazed out the window, happy that my current companion didn't need to talk. He was on his way to take me back to Sloane. A fresh wave of light passed over the car, and I leaned toward the window, struck by some sight.

There was a park across the street, bathed in moonlight, with a wide avenue of even lawn leading to a bench and a stone wall and a city vista. It called to me, for some reason unknown, and I asked my companion to stop the car. He looked at me curiously.

"Have somewhere to be?" I asked, one eyebrow raised quizzically. He shook his head and pulled up to the curb. I was out of the door before he had the car in park, my shoes left behind on the grass. He hurried to follow, and I put my hand in the crook of his elbow as we walked. It seemed the right thing to do. But it felt all wrong.

"This is quaint," my companion said with a chuckle. "Like some old make-out spot. Hey, er ..." he looked down at me in question.

"I don't think so," I said. "I'm done here. So are you."

I turned back toward the car, disillusioned. Whatever magic I'd hoped to find here, it was gone now.

—

"Time to go back, princess," Sloane said. "Sun's coming up."

"Just a minute," I said, my cheek pressed against the cold metal of my post. I could see that the sky was lightening to a pearl grey–rose. I didn't know why I waited, except that moving required too much effort. Or rather, it was a pointless exercise in a meaningless existence. Sloane seemed to catch my morbid mood, for he came up behind me and placed a worried hand on my back.

"I'm alright," I said quietly. I smiled humourlessly, knowing he wouldn't believe the lie. "Or, I will be."

"He's not ..." Sloane began, then caught himself as if in a dire blunder.

I turned on him. "He who? He's not what? I wish someone would tell me what on earth was going on!"

"L—Lucas wouldn't ..." Sloane stammered.

"I get it. Lucas doesn't want me to know. That much is apparent. But don't I have a right to know why I scream blue murder in my sleep, why I cry for nothing? Why I feel like I've lost the magnet in my compass?"

"I just meant to say *he*—the one you *feel* like you're waiting for—he's not coming. I just don't want you waiting for something that will never be."

"Thanks for the concern, Sloane, but I'm not waiting for any..."

I blinked. The dawn could be playing tricks on me, but I was sure something was going on with the light across the street. No, it wasn't just me, because Sloane was squinting, too, and then gawking.

It seemed brighter. Brighter by degrees each second. And as the sky grew lighter and the streetlights began to flicker out one by one, the space under this one burned brighter still, until I could barely look at it anymore. But I did, despite the searing pain. I searched the white hot light for the thing I'd been waiting for—the thing I knew was coming, somehow.

I thought I could discern some sort of pattern in the light—a tracery of interlacing lines that seemed at once alien and familiar. And then the pattern moved as if alive, like vines twisting and changing, until they resolved into a tall figure. The light gave a final, blinding pulse, and vanished, leaving behind a solid, flesh–and–blood person standing there.

I gasped, pushing away from the lightpost that had been holding me up and throwing off Sloane's grasping hands. I sprinted across the street. I didn't know yet what I was running to. But the compass that had lacked the needle now swung toward my true north and stayed as if pulled by the gravity of a thousand suns.

My eyes were recovering from the light, and I could see more and more by the moment. It was a man there, waiting. No, he was running too, arms outstretched for me. He knew me, and I knew him more surely than anything else I had encountered in the past few muddled days and nights. I saw his face, and suddenly everything was clear.

Cale!

We met in the middle of the street, crushing into each other's arms like lovers after a war. His lips were on mine, and he was lifting me from my feet.

"You were dead! You were dead! I saw it!" I cried between kisses, my tears free and my voice wracked with sobs.

"I was," he said with a radiant smile. He set me down on my feet, though the circle of his arms didn't break for a second.

"Why, Cale?" I demanded, the memories of that awful day bursting in on me with all the attendant anger, fear, shame, and sorrow.

"It was the only way," he said, holding my face in his hands and brushing my hairline with his thumbs. "Believe me, if there were any other way, I would have done it. I'll explain."

"Emma, you need to come!" Sloane called urgently from the sidewalk. I looked at him over my shoulder. He looked downright spooked. And I guessed he would be, seeing a man he'd watched Lucas shoot appear in a blast of light and stroll across the street.

"I'm not coming," I said with a sure smile. Whatever Cale had to explain, I knew the worst was over. Lucas had no power over me anymore. The very fact that I remembered Cale was proof enough of that. The Ambrosia had lost its effect. I would never have to live through another moment as Lucas's slave. It was done.

"Come with us," Cale called to Sloane.

Fear warred with longing across Sloane's face. I could tell he wanted to come, but he was afraid of what Lucas might do. He also feared what might happen if he returned without me. His indecision vanished and he cast his lot in with Cale.

With a shrug and a nervous laugh, he crossed the street. "There's nothing for me here, without you, princess."

"Funny you should call me that," I said with a laugh. I felt buoyant, held up by the strength of Cale's arms. "Shouldn't we be going?" I asked Cale. He seemed in no hurry to get away—not afraid of anything that Lucas could do to us now.

"One thing, first," he said, reaching for my hand and putting something cold around my finger. My ring. Tears filled my eyes as I remembered Lucas giving it back to him. I stroked his fingers, recalling the sickening crunch of the bones. I ducked my head, ashamed to look in Cale's eyes, but he lifted my chin gently.

"I have to know—do you love me?"

I let out a sob. "Of course I love you! I love you more than life! And I'm sorry, so sorry that I let you down."

"I warned you that you would," he said. "And it's okay. It was okay even then. I knew it had to be that way, or you would have been lost."

"And it was okay for me to think you had been lost?" I asked, dashing tears away from my eyes.

He smiled. "I told you, you know. When I gave you this. And other times." He ran a finger over my ring and kissed me.

I looked at him quizzically.

"Yes, I said that no matter where I go, I would come again without fail. For you."

"I remember now," I said, my eyes shining with tears. "But I didn't think anyone could come back from death."

"Do you not know me by now? Death can't stop me, my love."

"I should have known," I said wryly, with a laughing sob.

—

Cale whisked us away to the park where we had shared our last night together. Sloane came with us, looking decidedly nervous. He took up a post nearby to watch up and down the road as Cale brought me to our bench and pulled me close. His vigilance was useless, as any real threat to us would be invisible to Sloane's eyes, as well as mine. But Cale was so unconcerned, and I so secure in his arms, that I kept my opinion to myself.

"So, how did this happen?" I asked, not distracted for long. "You were dead—shot between the eyes. How did you come back?"

"When Lucas killed me, he thought he'd won. But he didn't count on one thing. Otherworld doesn't work the same way as this place. He never did take the time to understand the intricacies of Otherworld. When I came to this world, I became a part of it, even though I am still a true Otherworlder. I could have returned to Otherworld the way I came, but I would have relinquished my claim on you. So what I had done was irreversible, if I wanted to save you."

"So you had to die, to help me go back?" I asked, the truth dawning on me.

He nodded. "When I died, I took the fabric of this world into Otherworld and back again. It was the only way to join our worlds back together, and the only way to free you. I could go to Otherworld any time I wanted to, but you couldn't. By dying, I was able to open the door for you. That was only the beginning of my work.

"I immediately launched a battle against Lucas. He may have seemed a little strange to you, over the past few days? Yes, well, he was in the middle of a hand–to–hand battle for the world—and you. We fought it in Otherworld, in that clearing I warned you away from long ago in the pass of Rysha."

I remembered the place, in disturbingly vivid detail. I remembered the last of the sunlight before the complete, absorbing darkness of the wood of Iffreyn. I could see in my mind the twisted, stunted trees overshadowing the gateway of Rysha into Lucas's dark land where I betrayed Cale and lost my innocence. I felt again the terror and shame I had lived there, when Lucas had taken my crown and torn me away from Otherworld. It was there I had first tasted Ambrosia, there my slavery had begun. I shuddered at the memory.

Cale sensed my dark thoughts and rubbed my arm, reminding me that everything had changed now.

"And you won—you defeated him?"

"Yes," he said, closing his eyes with the sweetness of victory. He opened them again and looked at me. "Yes, I did."

I imagined him in his battle–dress, the sun glinting from his helm and his sword flashing, his white robes glowing as he fought at the head of his avenging army from the back of his mighty warhorse. I imagined dark Leyukas throwing down his banner in surrender, his weapons broken on the battlefield.

"Does this mean that I can go to Otherworld now?" I breathed. I thought of the lush valley of Parras, the white palace of Naeve, the breezy meadows and the quiet glades where I had lived with Kaehl so long ago. "Can I be your Immah again?"

He smiled, a little sadly, and my face fell. "Not yet," he said, kissing my fingertips. "We have a lot of work to do, still. Lucas is defeated, but he is not completely incapacitated. That time will come," he said, with a grim set to his jaw.

"Okay. I think I can wait—a little while," I smiled ruefully, remembering how my impatience had caused this catastrophe in the first place. But Cale had made it all right again. For the first time in my very long life, I had real hope.

"There's something you'll need for the job, too. Something I couldn't give you before." He smiled, and the world shifted. He was suddenly transformed, in his princely robes, with his shining crown and the light glowing from within him. I was changed, too, with my flowing hair and my white gown, and the weight of my own circlet resting on my head.

All around us, instead of the park was the mossy, blossoming hollow where Kaehl had made me. I gasped.

"I thought you said I couldn't go back to Otherworld yet," I cried, looking around in delight.

"You aren't actually there—you are seeing with Otherworld eyes."

As he spoke, I understood what he meant. I could see a faint glimmer, like a shadow of this world behind the lustre of Otherworld. It was a funny thing, to realize that everything I thought of as the "real" world was merely a shade, a flimsy counterfeit of the true world.

I looked closely at Cale, and I could see him both as he was here and in Otherworld at the same time. It was like the effect of my mirror, only now I wouldn't need to rely on a tiny polished square. My eyes would show me the truth now. My Otherworld eyes.

I wished I could stay in that hollow forever, with Cale. But the glimpse of home melted away, leaving us sitting in the park with a bewildered Sloane.

"What in the world was that?" he asked, blinking.

"You saw it?" I asked. Cale nodded with a wink.

"I let him have a look," he said. "He'll believe it better this way."

"It was nothing in this world, if you get my meaning," I explained. "It's my home, and yours, too, now."

Sloane was still bemused, but he gave a shrug and a laugh. "I must be crazy," he said, shaking his head.

"The visions will come and go," Cale said to me, kissing my eyes, "As you need them. Your sight won't seem complete, but you'll never be left blind."

"Thank you," I breathed. I saw that I was dressed normally now—or rather, that Cale had replaced my skimpy clothes with a pair of jeans and a white shirt, and my sword hung from a belt at my waist, safely invisible to all but Otherworlders. And I was a true Otherworlder, again, at last.

10

The days that followed were pure bliss. Mike and Gabe came and picked us up at the park, much to Sloane's alarm. But despite their intimidating appearance, they soon won him over and the three were my stalwart guardians and the best of friends. We drove out to the country again, to visit Simon and Annie, and Solomon. It was good to see them, the better still without Lucas's shadow hanging over us. I especially enjoyed seeing the fruits of our labour there, and the change Cale had brought to the town.

In contrast to our last sojourn, this visit was idyllic. Cale laid aside any kind of work, or practice, though we occasionally sparred with our swords for fun. We spent long hours together as we once had in Otherworld, hiking, riding through vistas that took on a faint cast of our Otherworldly haunts. Most of all, we enjoyed simply being together. And talking— always talking. He told me so much about Otherworld, what had transpired there in my absence and plans for the future. I confessed my fears and insecurities for the days ahead. He would give me advice, in return.

"You'll need to keep watchful," he would say, or, "Never forget who you are, and how much I love you."

"You'll be able to remind me," I said with a laugh. "Honestly, you talk like you won't be there."

Cale didn't respond, but ducked his head to examine a

tiny insect climbing a stalk of grass where we sat in the meadow.

"Please tell me you'll be there," I pleaded.

He gave me a faint smile. "I know it will be hard, but I will have to go."

"When?"

"Soon." He reached out and took me in his arms, stroking my back.

Sudden tears started in my eyes, and my throat grew tight. "When you died, I thought I had lost you forever. And then, when you came back...well, let's just say I was pretty happy to see you. I never thought, never wanted to be parted from you again. I thought we were in this together."

"We are. But this work, weaving our worlds back together, needs to be done from both ends. You from here ..."

"And you from Otherworld," I said glumly. "I get it."

"It won't be forever," he cajoled. "I will come back. Surely you can believe that promise, after all that's happened."

I nodded, coaxed into a little smile. It was true. If he could come back for me, as promised, from death, I could count on him to keep his word in any situation.

"And then we'll be married?" I asked, nuzzling into his neck.

"When the time is right."

I knew those words well. They had been an oft-repeated theme of our early days, and a point of contention that Lucas had identified easily as a weakness. But if nothing else, centuries of waiting for Cale had taught me patience. Time had a whole new meaning for me, now. This time, I knew better than to doubt those words.

—

It was an emotional send–off, the bunch of us on a hillside on Simon and Annie's estate. It was a capricious day, with a strong wind that was equally capable of blowing in a wild storm, or blowing the clouds away entirely. At the moment, it was settling for a bit of each—thick–piled clouds scudding across the sky, with streaks of sunlight falling so thickly between that they looked like solid curtains of gold. The ground was covered with spotted shadows that raced each other over the bright green meadows and the trees which were just starting to turn their leaves. The wind picked up my hair and twirled it in a wild bacchanalian dance around my head.

Cale held me in his arms, and not an eye was dry. Yet we all knew what he was going to do, and there was joy in the parting as well as sorrow.

"I wish it could have been a different way," I said softly next to his ear. We both knew what that meant, and the unspoken apology hung in the air between us.

"As long as you love me, my Emma, I wouldn't change a thing," he answered.

"Promise you'll come back?"

"Of course!" he avowed, kissing me deeply. "Never doubt it. But I'll be with you, in a way, even while I'm gone. Look for me, with your Otherworld eyes."

He gave me a vision now, and we were standing in the courtyard of his shining white palace, with all our people around. It was a great celebration, and I knew they could see me, too. A loud cheer went up, and music echoed from the walls. Our friends from my world were there, too, as they might have been in Otherworld. Sloane looked around in amazement at the alien sights, and I laughed in delight at his transformation, dressed in the garb of a courtier. Simon and Annie looked more at home, beaming at each other. They were young again, and at once I recognized Annie as my faithful lady-in-waiting, Annayeh.

"I should have known it was you!" I cried, embracing her.

Mike and Gabe, or rather Mikaehl and Gavreyl were back to their normal selves, as I had known them in my days as Princess. I had the feeling that they, too, were going home. I would be so lonely without all of them...especially...

I started weeping again and clung to Kaehl's robes. He looked down on me in compassion, as beautiful and noble and radiant as ever, and took my face in his hands.

"Not forever, my Immah," he said. "Soon, you'll be home, too."

He kissed me, long and deep with the passion and joy that can only precede parting. When his lips left mine, I kept my eyes closed for a long time. I knew when I opened them, he would be gone.

A thin, wrinkled hand slipped into mine, and Annie's voice spoke gently in my ear. "Come, child. He's not really gone, remember."

I opened my eyes to the empty space in front of me, on the windswept hillside where Sloane, Simon and Annie waited. The vision of Otherworld was gone, but I could almost hear the ghostly echo of the jubilant music, and feel the faint touch of a fingertip on my lips.

"I know," I said.

—

I drew my sword and nudged the door open with my foot.

With my Otherworld eyes, I saw two guards jump to the ready. But all it took was a quelling glare to put them in their places. They may not have feared me, on my own, but they knew whose banner I fought under.

I took a deep breath. I wasn't fearless, myself, by any stretch of the imagination. My heart was pounding, and I was shaking with nerves and adrenaline. But no one was going to know that. Besides, despite my fear, I knew the outcome of this encounter, and it gave me confidence I'd never before possessed.

I squared my shoulders, held my sword at the ready, and walked into Lucas Fulbright's office.

He looked up, in the middle of his morning transactions, and the look on his face was priceless. For a brief second, he was a mess of shock and horror. Then he schooled his features into that smooth, sinister set that used to intimidate me. I was amazed at how much I could see with my Otherworld eyes. I understood now how that unruffled steel was a front, a façade to hide how utterly afraid he was. I could almost pity him, except I knew the depths of his depravity and his boundless capacity for deceit.

"What brings you here, my Emma?" he purred with quick composure. "Do you need a fix?" He pushed a case of Ambrosia across the desk. "Or something more?" He leaned forward, his lips curving in seductive invitation, his eyes intense on mine. Once those tricks had worked on me, I admitted in consternation, but now I could see what I'd been blind to before—the tension at the corners of his mouth, the nervous flicker in his smouldering eyes. He was afraid, so afraid.

"You don't have anything I want," I said, my eyes flicking

to the Ambrosia with curious ambivalence. It tempted me, of course, with memories of enjoyable sensation. But there was no longer that pull, that need, that hunger for the drug. I could live without it. The realization surprised and pleased me, and I faced up to Lucas with renewed assurance. "You don't have me under your thumb anymore, and this time you know it's true. I'm not your Emma anymore."

I could feel that he was losing control. I heard the interested murmurs of some of the girls behind me, and even some of the men who weren't his Otherworld thugs, men like Sloane who were bound to Lucas through addiction, blackmail and threat. Lucas felt it too, and his fear turned dangerous.

I saw the unspoken signal Lucas gave, and my Otherworld eyes showed me the invisible warriors drawing close to me. They also showed me Cale's warriors—Mikaehl and some others—standing in my defence. I grinned at my champions, and raised my blade. Together, we fought them down with our swords.

"You see, I'm not afraid of anything you can do to me, anymore. You can't strike me, and nothing you can do will induce me to your side again. You've lost."

Lucas's mask slipped away entirely, and I saw the full force of his dread. With a smile, I extended the tip of my sword and casually knocked the case of Ambrosia onto the floor. I stepped up close to the desk, glaring at my enemy, and took great satisfaction in crushing the syringes under my heel.

Then I turned my attention to the hushed onlookers in the warehouse.

"You know me," I said. "I was once one of you. I was one of Lucas's slaves, just like you. But now you can see him for what he is, a pathetic, cowering loser. See that I am free, thanks to Cale. And if you want to be," I fixed my eyes on each of the people, "So are you."

With a last defiant glance over my shoulder at Lucas, I stalked out of the warehouse. Blinking in the rising sun's light, a few brave souls followed me out, into liberty.

—

So began my work here for Cale. Those rescued few were the first of many dear, courageous friends. I sent them, with Sloane, to Simon and Annie to heal for a while and then to train, as I did. Some rejoined me in the city, and some have travelled elsewhere, following the traces of Lucas's dark work everywhere it touches.

Lucas may be defeated, but he is not yet powerless. His cursed drug has made slaves of many—many of whom prefer the addiction even when they have seen me and others no longer dependent. I pity them, remembering how it felt when I measured my life by the gradients on the syringe. They have forgotten, as I had once, that they were made for Otherworld. This life is all they know.

I live in a little apartment in the city, now. Abby, my maid from my time in Lucas's apartment rooms with me. She's no longer mute—in fact, sometimes she talks too much. But she is a faithful friend and helper. We live in the shadow of Lucas's lofty penthouse, so whenever I look out the window, I am constantly reminded that although he seems strong, he will topple one day, when Cale comes back for me.

I think of Cale often. I miss him terribly. But, like Annie said, he is still with me. I see signs every day—I look for them everywhere with my Otherworld eyes. No matter how busy things get, no matter how inundated my apartment is with my new friends or how much there is still to be done, I take some time to go somewhere we've been together. Sometimes it's the little Italian restaurant, or the meadows and woods on Simon and Annie's estate, the diner where we had our first date, or the even the corner where I used to stand, where we met again for the first time. Right now, it's my favourite place, the bench in the park overlooking the city. -

I know why Cale liked this place. In a lot of ways, it reminds me of Otherworld—at least it's the best representation I might find in the city. But it also reminds me of all the work to be done, as if each glimmering light in the cityscape below is a person waiting to be freed, a strand waiting to be woven into the fabric of Otherworld.

I sigh and lean back on the bench, imagining Cale's arms around me.

"I wish you were here," I whisper aloud.

Beside my hand where it rests on the bench, I notice a faint shimmer in the wood. There is something drawn there, in shining, intricately traced lines—a heart with an arrow through it, the names *Kaehl* and *Immah* scripted within. As I watch, a word is etched beneath the heart. *Soon.*

Acknowledgements

First, to my Creator and the lover of my soul: thank you for putting this book in my mind—a place where a great many things get lost—and making sure I couldn't forget about it. This book is from you, for you, and about you first and foremost. I can't wait to be with you in "Otherworld".

Kevin: thank you for loving and supporting and shamelessly promoting me, and for teaching me so much about the beauty of perseverance and forgiveness. I love you.

Mom and Dad: thank you for encouraging my writing through the years, for the paper and the use of the typewriter/computer, and for being my first readers—especially Mom for the eagle eye. You were my first and best fans.

Thanks to all the teachers through the years who gave me great help and opportunities to grow in my writing skills—especially Mr. Kolumbus, Mrs. Doble, Mr. Lawrence, Mr. Brouse, Mr. Ritter, Mr. Greenfield, Mr. Compton and Brian Henry. Thanks Nathan for all the great sermons and bible studies during which I was writing this in my head, and for giving it a theological read–over. Thanks Warren for pointing me toward Word Alive Press. And thanks to the people at Word Alive who gave me this chance to share Christ's love with the world.

9 781770 692213